# RUNNER

# HAWK

Also by Michael Egan

Circles a Clover

Praise for *Circles a Clover*

'Haunting, intricate, gripping—there's a dark magic to the world Egan explores and well observed attention to the beauty and murk of the everyday.'

Jenn Ashworth, author of *Ghosted*.

**Michael Egan** grew up in Liverpool. He's a teacher, novelist and poet. Michael's poems have appeared in *Glasgow Review*, *Prototype* and *The Fortnightly Review*. His first poetry collection, *Steak & Stations*, was published by Penned in the Margins in 2011. In 2021 he was awarded the UEA Booker Prize Foundation Scholarship to study for an MA in creative writing and he gained a distinction. His first novel, *Circles a Clover* was published by Everything with Words in 2021. *Runner Hawk* is his debut for YA.

# RUNNER HAWK

# MICHAEL EGAN

EVERYTHING WITH WORDS

*Published in the UK 2023 by Everything with Words Limited*
*Fifth Floor, 30–31 Furnival Street, London EC4A 1JQ*

www.everythingwithwords.com

Text copyright © Michael Egan 2023.
Cover © Holly Ovenden 2023

Printed and bound in Great Britain by
CPI Group (UK) Ltd, Croydon CR0 4YY

A CIP catalogue record for this book is available
from the British Library.

ISBN 978–1–911427–36–0

for Claire

*as in the young-time, in the sap-years:*
*between the living floriations*
*under the leaping arches.*

from *The Anathemata* by David Jones

*The melody chord unwinds me,*
*the rhythm of life unties me,*
*brushing the hands of time away.*

from *Timeless Melody* by The La's

# *One*

It was right in a moment of stillness as the cold morning air bit at my breath that I first caught sight of the runner. He hung there in mid-stride, strange and unnatural in his frozen form. That morning I'd felt separated from everything that was going on around me. Standing still in that frost-covered field, I felt as if I'd been moving ahead of myself, as if part of me had been left behind while another part was beyond the *now* and the *past,* pushing into a future that wasn't mine. And I didn't care. I'd run out of time, but I didn't care.

There he was. His paused state taunting a snow-bound world. He wasn't possible but he was there. And looking at him, I had this feeling that I too was beyond time. Who I was seemed uncertain and unstable. I wasn't Leo Roslin watching a man who should have been way out of sight by now. Gone. I was without a name or a place. I was as impossible as that runner. My hand felt like a hand, but not my hand, not something intimately connected to me. Nothing was mine anymore. I called out. My voice was like an echo falling through a cave into a deep, too-complete silence, not like a voice at all. I couldn't have spoken. I hadn't reached out to touch the quiet and fill it with sound. I wasn't part of the same pulse that flowed through everyone else. Perhaps I never had been. I saw the runner, but I couldn't understand how he was possible and the more I looked at him, the more I felt like I was just the same as him. He'd run out of time, and now he was just stuck there. A ghost in the air.

Nothing that morning had been normal. For a start, I'd been running and that wasn't like me at all. I'm not someone who gets up at six in the freezing depths of winter and runs over fields for fun. I was running to get away from what my dad called my bone idleness. Get up, he kept telling me, do something with your life. I knew what he meant. He meant, Leo, you're seventeen, you need to find what it is you want to be. The looks of disappointment, the comments about what time I was getting up again, what time I was going to bed, was I even going to bed, the talk at dinner about his colleagues at work whose sons were off to university in the summer or had bagged some big-deal internship in London.

I couldn't give him what he wanted because the truth was, I had no idea how to do that. Everything felt like a dead end. Even when I tried to think about my future, about what I wanted, there was just this hollow space, that silence in the cave but this time without even an echo to pretend there hadn't always just been silence.

I think I ran because I wanted them to see me doing the one thing they wouldn't expect me to do. See that I wasn't inert. When I got up, Dad had been packing the car. They were going to Bermuda for Christmas because Dad's boss had offices out there. Not all work, but not completely a holiday either. We'd argued the day before. Dad shouting like he always seemed to shout when I couldn't give him the answer he wanted. I couldn't just say I know what I want, I can see it, I'll do it. I could only shrug and apologise, but even that seemed to make him hate me a little bit more. I was ungrateful. I was a waste of space. I was taking advantage of them. I was no son of his because a real son of his would have more get up and go. That had made Mum cry and though I'm pretty sure it was Dad's shouting that had upset her, he blamed me for her tears. I was upsetting her. I was letting him down. Did I even realise how lucky I was? It was only when Mum had run upstairs, shouting how could I know how lucky I was, that Dad stopped. There was this ugly quiet then in the dining room. It was heavy and suffocating. We sat there, finished our tea and then I got up and went to bed. I heard Mum crying from her room, but I didn't go to her. I slept. I did what they were accusing of me of doing. Nothing.

When I ran past Dad that cold morning as he packed the car with their suitcases, I didn't say anything. There was distance between us and I don't think either of us wanted to shorten that distance yet. He saw me and I saw his back straighten from the car boot, so I ran faster up our street and out of the village, away from him.

I only slowed down to a jog when I was out of Dad's sight. I ran up past The George and Dragon and then down past the church onto the footpath to Westage Lane. There was no one else around because it was so early on a Monday and so cold. I slipped a few times on the path but got my balance soon enough, found an unsteady rhythm on the potholed lane, and eventually I turned off Westage Lane and walked down Hield Lane to where it hit Dark Lane. There was another path there through some fields that led to the lake at Pick Mere. I think I'd half-decided to run as far as the lake though I never got there.

The air felt sharp as I breathed in. I stopped at the gate that led into the field and breathed in the air. Little ice knives stabbed into my lungs. A car whizzed past, too fast probably with the way the ice lay thick on the ungritted road. I dipped my chin into the collar of my jacket, so it covered my mouth, and pushed through the gate. There was a trickle stream frozen solid, and all the grass was white. My chest was burning though I'd hardly run. I walked on a little across the field. I felt that satisfying shattering of frozen grass beneath my boots. Every now and again I stopped, stamped my feet to break the ice and then stepped back, looked at the result of my stamping, dipped my toe against the ice and pushed it down so the black water beneath came up.

I hadn't been walking long when I saw the runner. Pick Mere was still a way off, but my chest was aching from the run. Dad was probably right, I was a layabout, because I was out of breath, and I'd hardly been running for long. I was half considering turning around, not bothering with carrying on to the mere, when I saw him.

The field rose a little and there he was on its crest. At first, I thought he was stretching or just taking a breath. It was a cold day after all, my own chest was still burning even though I was no longer running. I stopped and watched him. He wasn't exactly equipped for the conditions either. He was wearing a shiny green tracksuit, like the kind people wore in the eighties. It had a blue stripe down each arm and each leg.

He didn't have a hat on to fight off the cold or any gloves for that matter. That was strange but then I'd seen runners round here in the depths of winter in vests and shorts. Then I noticed how his body was held, one leg back and lifted from the ground, one arm forward stretching out, one arm back. The morning sun was glaring down, so I brought my hand up to shield my eyes. I could see he wasn't moving. He was running but it was almost as if he had been frozen in the act of running, mid-stride, mid-jog. I kept watching him, expecting him to suddenly run, as if this were a kind of joke he was pulling on someone who might be watching him, on me. It was as I watched him, so unmoving and unreal, that I began to feel myself pulling away, separating from the world, being stretched out of belonging into isolation. I was as numb as he was. As disconnected from the world. I stared at him and the more I stared, the more I forgot who I was, why I was. I don't know how long I stood there for, but he didn't move once in all that time. Frozen, though surely the day wasn't that cold, and surely if he was frozen, he would have toppled, fallen to the grass.

Like a string had suddenly snapped I felt my body shudder, as if it had only just remembered how cold the day was, remembered to feel something. I shoved my hands in my pockets. Standing in one place had made me feel the cold more. I shivered, jumped up and down. Still, he didn't move an inch. I kept watching him, suddenly entranced again. I knew I was standing just as still as he was. I knew that time was moving and that nothing was changing, but I stayed there, watching him. And within that stillness, so complete and unnatural, I felt separation, as if part of me had stretched far beyond my standing place and was gone.

I almost called to him. I had no idea what I would have called. *Hello there? Are you okay? Hey, mate, what's wrong with you?* But I didn't say anything in the end. Eventually, I pulled my hands from my pockets and made myself turn away. I walked back towards Dark Lane trying to forget about him. Whoever he was, it was obvious he wasn't right, that there was something strange about him, but I didn't want to think about him too much, because if I started on that, really thinking about what I'd just seen, I'd be forced to admit I'd seen something impossible and inevitably I'd try to make sense of that, make it possible.

As I walked along Dark Lane and onto Hield Lane then down the path and back into Great Budworth, I locked him away in a part of my brain where he could be forgotten. As I walked, I started to feel separated from everything around me again. I wasn't running. I don't think I could have. My body felt heavy, reluctant. Slow-stepping, too aware of the icy pavement, I was moving almost like a robot, my movements not my own. My hands were cold, numb. I couldn't hear a sound in the world. Even when a car passed me, I didn't hear a thing. I was only conscious of the car's shape passing me, moving beyond me. It could have taken me a few minutes to get back into the village or it could have taken me a year. I couldn't tell the difference. It was only as I came down towards the church and heard the girl singing that I was brought back into myself. That separation, that disconnect the runner had initiated, vanished as soon as I heard her voice. I heard an engine start in the pub car park. Birds called at the slow-waking morning. My phone buzzed in my pocket. I heard the girl sing.

# *Two*

The girl was standing at the church doors. I don't think I'd ever seen her before or at least I didn't recognise her, but I knew the vicar had a daughter. Everyone knew that because everyone knew he used to have two daughters but the older one had vanished a few years ago. Mum told me once she'd run off with an older boyfriend, that one of the women who helped clean the church had told her she was probably in Australia, that it was only to be expected because of how the daughter used to clash with her dad. Apparently, she was wild, and the vicar was anything but wild. She was bound to break free someday, that's what Mum said, and I think what everyone thought. There was no mystery, no sinister reason for her vanishing. She was eighteen after all, free to do as she liked. She'd run away, that was all there was to it.

The girl at the church doors must have been younger than me because she was wearing a school uniform, a navy blazer, tartan skirt, and snow-white blouse but no tie. It was the uniform of the private school down the road. She was leaning against the doors looking off into the graveyard, humming when before she'd been singing, not even aware I was passing. Her leg was tapping against the stone path. She had her red hair tied back and was shivering, pushing herself as close to the door as she could.

I kept walking down the hill back towards my house. As I passed the graveyard, I could still hear her humming. Soft, low, mixed in now with the song of the birds in the bare trees.

As I walked down High Street, I could see how pretty the village looked covered in snow and with the clear blue of the winter sky above. It's strange where I live. For a start, Great Budworth is probably one of the most beautiful villages you could live in. I mean it, it's ridiculously quaint. Sometimes I think that if you grabbed any random American tourist from somewhere like Elk Bend, Idaho, and asked them to draw an English town, like a proper picture-postcard village, they'd draw something exactly like Great Budworth. It's insanely picturesque and that morning it looked just like a postcard. An image trapped in time.

Dad was standing at the driver's side of our car, arms folded across his jumper, trying to smile. He hadn't shaved for days so he had a mess of stubble that was threatening to form a tatty beard. That didn't look right on him. Dad was always clean shaven, immaculate, but there he was in a scruffy old jumper, his thinning hair brushed back and slicked down with too much gel.

I could see Mum in the passenger seat, motionless, almost like she wasn't Mum, like she was a Mum-shaped doll just propped up there playing at being Mum. I wondered if she was still upset with me from the night before.

Dad frowned, his face heavy with what I took to be the strain between us, but might have only been tiredness at such an early start.

We thought you might have run off without saying goodbye, he said.

I looked at Mum. She was there in the passenger seat, staring ahead though there was nothing on the street but the quiet emptiness of morning. It was like she didn't even know I was there.

It was much lighter out now, the sun burning yellow over The George and Dragon, and yesterday's snow still clinging to the pavement, compacted and stubborn.

I just needed to get out for a bit, I said.

Dad laughed. It was an effort, that laugh, as if he were trying as hard as he could to thaw the tension. No harm in that, he said. Anyway, we're about ready to get off.

He moved towards me, put a gloved hand on my shoulder.

Go on in, he said and though his hand was on my shoulder it wasn't like he was holding my shoulder. He just let his hand rest there.

Your mum's dog-tired, not even sure she's awake, you know how she gets in the morning. You go on in, Leo. Get yourself back to bed. We'll ring you when we get to the airport.

I'm sorry, I said.

Dad smiled again. It was a sad, forced smile. I'm sorry too mate, he said.

I looked round him to my mum. I'm not a baby, it wasn't like I needed Mummy to kiss me goodbye, but I had this feeling that I needed to say goodbye to her or that it was just wrong to not say goodbye. But she was still just gazing forward, unaware of anything else. I couldn't even tell if her eyes were closed because the windshield was cloudy with slowly warming ice.

Dad's hand left my shoulder.

Will you tell Mum I love her? I said.

That wasn't something I said every day. I'm not a bad son.

I don't go round telling my parents I hate them or ignore them. I just don't like saying a type of thing like *I love you*. I prefer showing that love. I do the dishes. I keep my room clean. In summer I mow the lawn. I even cooked a meal for their anniversary this year. I'm a good son, I know I am, I'm just not vocal with that love on a daily basis.

Dad patted my arm. She knows you do, he said. Now go on, off you go. We'll call you.

Something weird happened then. My dad is a man's man. Not much emotion unless he's watching Crewe play and then that's usually an emotion full of swear words and disappointment. He's worked all his life in tough, high-pressured jobs. He started out in a factory when he was sixteen, no qualifications. He told me he couldn't even read until he was twenty because no one had diagnosed his dyslexia when he was at school. But then after he met Mum, she got him a job at a place called Foresight Nickson, this big technology firm out near Winsford. That's when Dad started getting his promotions. One after another. Mum always said Dad was well-liked, that he was a man other men instantly respected, not one they feared or were jealous of. After I was born, he climbed his way to financial manager at Foresight Nickson and when I was three, we were able to move to a massive townhouse in Great Budworth. But all through my life, even though he's been a good dad, played football with me, read to me, taught me to shave, gave me *that* talk, he's never told me too often that he loves me, and he's never hugged me let alone kissed me. But that morning, his hand moved from my arm to my cheek and he kind of pulled me towards him. I bowed my head, it felt so strange to be so close to him and within this sudden showing of love. I could smell old aftershave on his jumper. I felt his stubble against my hair. He kissed my head and pulled me close to him.

We love you, Leo, he said and kissed me again.

He let go of me, almost as if he'd suddenly remembered he was, after all, a man's man and that kissing me was an unnecessary show of emotion. He stepped abruptly back, gave my hair a tussle like he used to when I was five, then turned and joined Mum in the car.

I think I stood there for about ten minutes before I realised they'd driven off. I was just stood on our doorstep in the freezing morning. It was only the slow roll of another car's wheel that pulled me back to reality. I shivered. My body was ice despite the fact I was wearing a thick jacket and tracksuit bottoms. I went inside and shut the door, locked it. I leaned against the door and even though Mum and Dad had only just left, even though nothing had really changed about our house, the hallway and the stairs and closed kitchen door felt different. The house felt empty, too quiet. I'm not saying I felt scared being alone, it wasn't that at all. It just felt like something had been lost, that the sounds that I'd always known would fill my home, the feel of its space even when Mum and Dad were working or Dad was in the garden, had gone somewhere else. I know how crazy that was. They'd only gone on holiday. But as I stood against the door, it felt like something had been lost that wouldn't ever come back.

# *Three*

That first day, I did exactly what Mum and Dad would have expected me to do. I wasted it sleeping and playing FIFA. It was nearly midnight before I realised I hadn't eaten. They'd left plenty of food for me. The fridge was stocked full of steak, chicken, cheese, milk, vegetables and even a few of Dad's German beers. My parents used to be very strict about my health, there were very few things they'd let me eat and most of that was usually as vegan as you could get. But in the last few months they seemed to have done a complete flip. I didn't even eat meat properly until I was fourteen but since last summer it had been either steak or chicken for tea. Protein, protein, protein. It was as if Mum had decided I was getting weaker as I got older which was nuts because if anything I was too skinny when I was younger. I'm not saying I exercise loads, but I did sit-ups every day and walked an excessive amount, so I'm not exactly a waif anymore.

I didn't cook any of the food. I ate Wotsits, maybe about six packets, sat on the living-room floor with the lights dimmed, eating the crisps, and drinking Dad's beers. After four bottles, I felt more anxious than drunk. It was like I suddenly knew I was alone. I jumped up and went to the back door, checked it was locked, then the same to the front. I went into Mum and Dad's room and made sure it was empty, then mine, then the spare rooms, dad's office, then the kitchen and dining room, even the cellar. I raced round the house, my stomach swirling with Wotsits and Erdinger. It was only after I was done that I knew it wasn't because I was afraid. That wasn't what I'd been feeling. Not fear. I've been home alone before. It was more that I wanted to know I was completely alone, almost like I was safe in the cocoon of the house, and no one could come in to ruin that. Mum and Dad hadn't even called but I didn't care. Them not calling was part of that enclosed separation. This space was mine, the house was mine, and until my Uncle Toby came to visit as he'd promised, whenever that would be, I could do what I wanted. If that meant living on Wotsits and Erdinger then that's what I'd do.

I came back to the living room and lay on the carpet,

looking up at Mum's new lampshades. They were four glass shades, each at different lengths, each a different pastel colour, soft pinks and blues. I put a Wotsit against my lips and let it stay there as I stared at the lampshades. With one hand I reached for the remote, and without sitting up I put Spotify on the television. I didn't care what played. I just went to a playlist and hit play. It must have been Dad's playlist because Ride's *Vapour Trail*, flushed out the living room's silence. I knew that song. Dad would play it over and over in his car when I was little. I stared at the lampshades as the song played. The glass moved slightly, swaying though there was no breeze in the room. I could see dust dancing in the dimmed light, dust layered upon the contours of the glass. When was that memory of listening to that song from? I knew I was very little, a toddler maybe, but it was such a vivid memory that as I lay on the couch, I thought it was a memory I must be making up. You don't remember things from that long ago, that clearly, do you? That's insane, humans aren't computers. You remember things like that because you've seen them in photographs and think they're memories, so they become memories. I have a clear memory of sitting on a seesaw with our old Springer, Chet. But that isn't a real memory. It's from a photograph that Mum has in a little frame on a unit in the dining room. I don't see that photograph all the time, or at least I don't notice it, so the captured memory, the photograph, has become an imagined memory. Maybe that was what the song was like. Maybe there was a picture of me somewhere in the house showing me sitting in the back of Dad's car and maybe when it was taken, I was listening to *Vapour Trail* because that's a song he would have been playing.

The lampshades kept moving. Slight. Barely perceptible. I blew the Wotsit away from my lips, so it rolled down my chin, down my throat to rest on my collar bone. I put my hand up as if it could reach the lampshades, stop them moving. Maybe I was a bit drunk, but the truth is sometimes when I'm alone I get these weird thoughts, like for instance I used to imagine I could levitate even though I knew I was only standing on tiptoes, and a few years ago, not anymore, I used to think if I concentrated hard enough, I could push my hand through solid objects. I practised that on my wardrobe and on the banisters, even on a stack of books. It never worked but that didn't stop me believing it might work one day.

I lay there, reaching up to the lampshades, made my fingers splay out as if I could grab the glass shades and make them stop. But I couldn't.

The lampshades kept swaying. Then something else

happened. I wanted to bring my arm back down, to relax my fingers, but my hand refused to listen. It had gone tight, the fingers like stone. They were so set in place they almost hurt, as if the fingers were trying to pull apart from each other so that every time I tried to make them close, they only fought back to stay spread. It was a kind of stalemate between my will and my hand.

Stuff like that has happened before to me. When I was about ten, Mum and Dad took me to a doctor. He did all kinds of tests. I remember Mum worrying about epilepsy because sometimes my hands would spasm and I think I had a kind of fit once though it didn't last long. She needn't have worried. I hated the doctors, the few visits to the hospital near Crewe, the poking and prodding, feeling like there was something hidden inside me that was broken or damaged, waiting to be revealed and categorised. It took weeks. I remember seeing Mum crying all the time. In the end it was Dad who took me for the appointments. In the car to the hospital, we'd talk about anything other than the fact we were going to hospital. Football. Marvel films. Fishing. Even his work which I didn't understand. Every time we got to the hospital he'd park the car, turn to me and say, here we go again then. But that was the only reference he'd ever make to what was happening. Even in hospital, we'd sit there in silence until my name was called. And afterwards he'd take me through Sandbach for a McDonalds, and we'd be back to talking about football and anything except where we'd just been. I know that might all make my dad sound like he didn't care but that's not true. If anything, he helped me push the worry away, helped me get through those weeks. I think being within the close influence of his stubborn stoicism must have washed off on me. I learnt to believe that there was nothing wrong, so everything couldn't be anything but okay.

After a few weeks, the tests all came back clear. Dad had been right, there was nothing wrong with me at all that could be neurological, not a hint of anything like epilepsy to worry about. Mum stopped worrying. Dad never mentioned our trips to hospital. I'm not saying I never had anything else strange happen. Any shakes or times when I felt like I couldn't move. All of that did keep happening. I just didn't let anyone know it was happening. The doctors had been explicit in their diagnosis. There was nothing physically wrong with me, so when Mum and Dad believed whatever had been wrong had passed, put it down to age or growing up, I didn't want them to start believing there was something still wrong. Something deeper, more hidden. I didn't want to believe that either. Whenever my hands started to shake a little, I'd go to my room, shut my door and wait until whatever was going on had passed. In that way I started to believe what Mum and Dad believed. There was nothing wrong with me.

I don't know how long I stayed there, looking up at my frozen hand, ordering my arm to come back down, begging my fingers to close into a soft fist. I think I might have cried a little but that didn't matter, there was no one to see me cry. My arm ached. My fingers felt like they weren't my fingers, like they weren't even fingers. Concrete, absent, foreign. I thought I'd be there all night but at last my arm just fell to the carpet like the string holding it up had been suddenly severed. I didn't move. I just stayed there, breathing, feeling sensation flood back into my numb arm and hand. Pins and needles came first, then the fingers were twitching. But I still didn't get up or even bring my hand close to me. I just lay there.

That type of thing keeps happening to me. If it's not my hand, it's my leg hanging mid-stride, or when I'm brushing my teeth, I'll just freeze and look at myself in the mirror, toothpaste dripping from my mouth, unable to swallow. It's even happened when I'm drinking a glass of Coke so that the Coke keeps pouring down my throat until it's coming out of my mouth and all over my chest, but I can't do anything to make my hand move the glass away. I don't understand it. I don't want it. But it keeps happening and each time it happens, it lasts a little longer. Sometimes, I worry that one day I'll just freeze up completely, that my whole body will calcify and become a statue, stone forever, not one bit of me flesh. I tell myself that it's made up, all in my imagination, like the levitating, but I know it's not. This was real. This was happening. Every day I could feel my body lessening, stiffening. I hadn't told a soul, not even Toby. Not Mum or Dad. But lying there on the living room carpet, it felt like even though my hand was slowly waking up, that my waking state wasn't once again my natural state. I felt like this relief was temporary, that I was temporary, and that soon it wouldn't just be my hand freezing, it would be every part of me.

# *Four*

By the third day I thought if I didn't make myself get out and do something, I might end up locked away like some crazy recluse for weeks. I'd watched pretty much all my favourite films. I watched *Inception*, *Interstellar*, *Whiplash*, *Ex Machina*, *Inside Llewyn Davis* and, because Mum and Dad weren't there, *The Wolf of Wall Street*. I even binge watched all of Season One of *Succession*. By mid-afternoon, I got wrapped up because it had been snowing all morning and decided to go for a walk. It was one of those crazy winter days where the skies are clearer and bluer than any summer day, but your teeth are chattering as soon as you walk outside and the sun is this massive burning orange ball low on the horizon, sitting there all day as if it can't be bothered to rise too high because it knows its heat won't do anything to chase away winter's grasp.

I put on my walking boots because I had this thought I might try to find the runner. I think I wanted to know for certain that he hadn't been real and then maybe if I knew, then how he'd made me feel wouldn't be real either. Couldn't be real. I'd thought about him even though I'd tried not to. His stillness was so unnatural. He was like an apparition that wasn't in any way frightening but carried with it a haunting sense of absence. I think I wanted to see him move. Even if it was just that I stood at the edge of the field and saw him running, just as he should have been that day, then I think I could have forgotten about him. He wasn't a ghost. He wasn't impossible. He was just a broken moment and if I could see him again then that moment would be fixed.

Around our village it's all very rural, fields and farms, but we're not far from Northwich and that's an ugly town. There's this horrible power plant that sometimes seems almost beautiful out near Lostock. Whenever we drive past that place it feels like I'm in a dystopian city in some toxic future. It all looks so broken, like it shouldn't have ever been put there. There are rusty pipes criss-crossing over the street. Some mornings there's a haze that comes up from the river and rests in the dip so it's like a thick, sick fog. I wonder sometimes if that fog is natural, just trapped river mist, or if it's something worse seeping out of all the pipes that scar the place. It's so horrible it's perfect in a way. Sometimes I walk down past the power plant and, even though I don't think you're allowed, I go into this field that kind of looks like a moor, the grass vivid green, sheep everywhere, and I climb up on this ridge and look down on the power plant and maybe smoke a cigarette or two and just watch that place. There never seems to be anyone there. It's eerie and has an abandoned feel but Dad says it's just a chemical plant, working, employs loads of people in the area. I never see that. I always just see this concrete and steel hollowness. But I didn't want to walk that way that day. That way seemed too lonely, empty. I wanted to go into the fields and be part of the world even if there was no one else there. That wasn't lonely. Even when I walked alone through the fields near where I live, I never felt truly alone. If anything, I felt surrounded, observed, known.

But I was alone when I got to the field. The day felt the same. the same crisp grass that cracked beneath my boots. The same low sun. The same vast blueness of sky. The same deep cold that found its way into me the moment I stopped walking and stood at the gate.

The runner wasn't there.

I waited. I could feel time pass. Too slow, minute ached

into minute but there was only the empty field. No runner. No unmoving statue. I knew no matter how long I stayed there that he wouldn't come. In the end, I pushed the gate open and walked back along the lane towards the village. I don't know how people feel when they see a ghost, but I felt almost cheated as I walked home. It was like I'd gone back into the haunted house but all the feeling of being haunted had vanished. No ghost, no answers. Just the gnawing thought that I'd imagined everything, that there was something wrong with me, that even the act of going back into the house had been enough to prove my own madness. I had seen nothing. I would see nothing again.

When I passed the old post office, I saw there was a red Jensen Interceptor parked outside the house. It was a car I'd been in a dozen times. I'd even driven it last summer.

When I came to our front door, I didn't need to unlock it. I pushed it open and saw an army issue holdall left at the bottom of the stairs and a Borg jacket tossed over the banister.

Look what the cat dragged in, said a familiar voice.

Uncle Toby was stood in the kitchen doorway, a beer in one hand. He was much younger than Mum, not far past thirty, but he looked like her twin. The same blue eyes, the same Greek nose inherited from their dad. His hair was longer than the last time I'd seen him, and he was wearing a navy suit like he'd just come from a wedding.

I smiled. Wow, you've come back at last. I suppose I should slaughter a fatted calf or something.

Toby grinned. Nah, Roslin. Didn't you hear the news? No need for sacrifices anymore. God is dead and all the angels couldn't give a shit.

# Five

So, come on, Roslin, said Toby. What's the story?

That was Uncle Toby's code for *I know I've been away for a while but I'm back now, let's pretend we saw each other yesterday.*

I love my Uncle Toby, I do. But the truth is we hardly see him anymore. That's not all his fault. Since he got a job at Goldsmiths teaching Literature, he's been swamped in that whole London life. Of course, there's his poetry too. Toby Saravakos is a pretty big deal in poetry. He was a Guardian Next Generation Poet last year and his first collection, *Barbarian*, was shortlisted for the TS Eliot Prize, while his second, *Savage Horizon*, won the Forward Prize. I'm not sure what any of that means exactly, but as far as poets go, I think that makes him as famous as it gets. I looked at his *About* page on the Picador website a few weeks ago. It says he's the working-class heir to Cavafy. I know who that guy is. He's a Greek poet from years ago who used to live in Liverpool just like Mum and Toby. But I wouldn't call Toby working class, not anymore. Just like Mum, he's flushed out his Liverpool accent. Mum went for generic Cheshire, whereas Toby has gone for bourgeoise Londonista. I'm no Marxist, but I think it's sad when people toss away their past like that, hide it, cover it with a different skin. It's all just a mask, isn't it? I'm never going to be like that, who I am is who I am, and I don't want to ever have to pretend I'm someone I'm not. Somewhere underneath the Sky Arts, *TLS, I know the commissioning editor of Faber*, Uncle Toby is the Toby Saravakos who grew up on Cawdor Street, Toxteth, in a tiny house no one lives in anymore, dreaming of playing for Everton, not writing 'urgent, modern and essential prose poetry'. But don't get me wrong, I'm not attacking him. I love him, I really do, it's just I wished he could be honest from time to time.

Same as always, I said. Except I've been abandoned. I'm technically an orphan now.

We were sat in the living room. Toby in Dad's armchair, me on the arm of the sofa. Toby had put music on, some jazz I didn't really mind but couldn't be bothered asking who it was. Toby was on his second beer; he'd shoved one in my hand but I was only sipping it. I kept thinking of that runner, wondering if he was still out there on the field, unmoving, trapped. Could a person really freeze solid like that? Should I have called an ambulance or something? I saw this film once called *Jindabyne*. It wasn't very good even though the cinematography was nice and subtle, and Australia looked pretty in it. It's a sad film about these men who go on a fishing trip and find a girl's dead body. They know she's been murdered, but they don't do anything. They just tie her to something so her body doesn't float away and go on with their trip. It's the most selfish thing I've ever seen in a film. I don't really remember much else about the film or what happened in the end, but I remember how weird I felt watching the men just go on with their lives. I thought to myself I'd never do anything like that, but then I'm sure that's what everyone thinks. Maybe that was the point of the film, to make everyone reflect on who they think they are, who they really are. But wasn't I just like those men? I'd left the runner out there. What if he was in trouble? What if he was still out there, alone and lost? The strange thing was, amongst all that guilt, there was another stabbing thought that was getting stronger the more I thought about what I should have done. Surely the man wasn't real. It didn't make sense that a man could just be frozen mid-stride like that.

And why was he wearing clothes from years ago? Nobody wears tracksuits like that anymore. What was he? A time-traveller stuck in the moment of crossing time's boundaries? That was ridiculous. No, it was more rational to believe that he was all in my imagination. That there was no runner, and therefore no need for me to get help for him and no need for me to feel guilt.

You're not a sodding orphan, you dimwit, said Toby, sinking into the armchair. You're nearly eighteen. Jesus, do you know what I would have given to be alone for a few weeks when I was eighteen?

But I bet you had friends, a girlfriend, I said.

Toby swigged his beer. Don't give me that self-pitying crap. You're better than that. You're a good looker, Roslin. If I took you down to London, half my students would be after you. It'd be a feeding frenzy and you'd be the prime meat. So don't give me your sob story about loneliness and lovelessness. You've just not lived all that stuff yet, but I'm telling you, if you only had the chance, my God you'd live it more than any of us.

He laughed to himself and, though I thought he was going to keep speaking, he just kind of trailed off, stared up at the mantelpiece where there was a photo of me in Mum's arms when I was a baby. He stood up, went to the mantelpiece, put his beer down next to the photograph then picked the photograph up.

Look at you, he said. You're the spitting image of your mum. Look how happy she is. Eighteen, Leo. Eighteen, my sweet God.

He laughed again.

I don't feel it, I said. I feel like a kid, like I know I'm nearly eighteen, but it feels like there's a chunk missing. Did you think that when you were eighteen? Like you'd got there too fast?

Toby put the photograph down and looked at me. He never looked worried. His blue eyes were always bright like the sky that morning. Alive and lacking any doubt that life was amazing. But as he stood at our mantelpiece there was a little gap in that joy, I could see it. A little dimming in that brightness. It might have been nostalgia. I hate nostalgia. Last week I was making bulgogi with Mum and she was grating pears into the marinated meat while I was slicing some onions when she just put down the grater and the pear and came over to me. She held me. Then she pulled away and took my face in her hands. I could smell soy, gochujang, and pear juice on her fingers.

Where did my best boy go? she said. Where did the years go, Leo?

I didn't know what to say. I just let her hold my face and stare at me. It was a little crazy, made me feel uncomfortable, but I thought maybe if I pulled away that would just make her sadder, like that was what a man would do, not her best boy. Her best boy would let her hold him. That's nostalgia, isn't it? Nostalgia for the child Mum used to love, the one who relied on her for everything. I'm sure that's natural, that every parent feels that, so I didn't resent her for it. I just let her have her moment.

No way, said Toby. I was absolutely ecstatic to be eighteen. Anyway, I think I'd been eighteen since I was ten, so actually being eighteen just gave me permission to live like an eighteen-year-old. You know what I did?

I shook my head. Got pissed?

That too, he said. But first, I got the bus from Toxteth up to Bootle. That's where your grandad lived with his new family. I went right up to his door. For some reason I knew he'd be in, and I knew he'd answer. And you know what I did when he answered?

I shook my head again.

I punched him. My God, Roslin, I could box when I was young. I get that from my dad at least. I used to go every week to a club in Anfield, so when I hit him, I really hit that bastard. Knocked him right out. His new wife, Scary

Mary me and your mum called her, she started screaming and saying she'd call the police, but my dad, give him credit, he waved her off, said something like leave the lad, and I stood over him, told him if he ever came near me or your mum again, I'd kill him. Crazy thing is, I think I meant it. I really do. I think back then I was so angry with him and life and what had happened to your nan, that I was capable of anything. Thank Christ he didn't come near us again and thank Christ I got out of Liverpool.

That's pretty intense, I said. I'd heard these stories before. How Grandad was with Nan. How he was with Mum. How he was with Toby. I got it, he was a terrible man.

Toby laughed. Intense, yeah. Everything was intense then. So no, to answer your question. I felt like I'd lived all my years, too many of them. When I got to eighteen, I just felt like I had permission to really live them. You should feel that too. You've lived Leo. Remember that.

It doesn't feel like it, I said. Sometimes it feels like I haven't done anything, just been stuck here with Mum and Dad.

You needed to make friends that's all.

I sipped my beer. I will. I know I will, but it doesn't feel like there's anyone round here who I could be friends with.

Now is not forever, Roslin. Things change. What about a girl?

I shrugged.

A boy?

No, I mean I'd want a girl if I wanted anyone. But there's no one here.

I see that, kid. But maybe you haven't looked properly. Have you even been out past the village since all that stuff happened?

I frowned. There was a gap in my brain, I could feel it as soon as he said 'stuff'. If someone says to you, do you remember that time we went to Alton Towers or do you remember the Sunday dinners your nan used to cook, you see it in your mind don't you, you have this flash, glimpse it. It's there. It exists again just for a fragment of a second. But when Toby spoke there was no flash. No brief memory. No spark. Just emptiness.

What stuff?

Toby took another drink of his beer and went back to the armchair. He sat, leaning forward, looking at me super intensely.

Come on, Roslin. You know what I'm talking about. What happened at Marbury?

I was still blanking. There was nothing. Even the

word Marbury, a word I knew meant the big country park with the lake just down the road, sparked only an absence. I couldn't even picture driving up to the park, parking up, walking the loop, the aviary, the steps. None of it. I knew they existed, but I couldn't make them pop into my mind like little polaroid pictures, flash, flash, flash.

I don't know, I said, but my words were kind of mumbled, strained.

It's okay, Roslin, said Toby and he wasn't looking at me so intensely now. He looked worried for once. I know you don't, he said. But maybe if I talk to you about it, that'll help you remember and then we can think about why it happened.

Why? I said. I don't know why, I mean I don't know what you're talking about.

I was holding my beer in my right hand but somehow I'd held it out as if I was giving it to Toby even thought I wasn't. I wanted the beer. My hand had just decided to hold it out, frozen like the runner. It was almost as if the strain of searching my brain for the memory of Marbury had made me cease up.

You were at the park with your mum and dad. Do you remember?

I shook my head. Of course, I remembered. I knew I had hundreds of memories of being at Marbury with Mum and Dad. How many times had we been there on a Sunday afternoon or in summer when we took a picnic and a football? I knew those memories existed because the events had existed, but all of Marbury was a hollow in my remembering.

I can't remember, I said. My words were slow. My Grandad Roslin, Dad's dad, had a stroke when I was fifteen. I went to visit him in hospital in Cardiff and though he was fine, alive, sitting up in bed, when he spoke his words struggled to keep up with what he wanted to say, and his mouth seemed to have forgotten how to even form them. I felt like Grandad Roslin as Toby looked at me with this stupid worried face that didn't suit him. I wanted to shout at him to leave me alone, that there wasn't anything that had happened at Marbury, that if there had been I'd remember it, I'd know what he meant.

You were with your mum and dad near the lake, he said. It was like he was telling me my memory, and the minute he gave me that image, me standing by the lake with Mum and Dad, I started to see it. Like his words were a trigger or the memory was being downloaded into me through his words.

It was summer, he said. The August bank holiday. You'd walked ahead to the point your mum and dad couldn't see you anymore. There were trees blocking their view, but you were still by the lake, and there was a little boy all by himself. He was feeding the ducks. Do you remember? He was about eight.

I nodded. I could see the boy. He had on a Man City top and shorts, his feet bare, and he was leaning over into the lake.

He was going to fall in, I said because I saw it then. I saw it like I saw it on the day. He was leaning too far over. Desperate to give a scrap of bread to one duck who hadn't had any yet. He was going to fall, I knew it, there was no doubt in my mind that he was going to fall in. I had to save him.

Yeah, he was going to fall in, said Toby. So, you ran to him and just as he was about to fall, you grabbed his arm. Do you remember?

I did. I saw it. My hand grabbing his arm. And he'd screamed. At first, I thought he screamed with fright, with that moment of realisation that something bad was about to happen as the water came rushing towards him, but then I understood it wasn't fear, it was pain.

I was holding him too tightly, I said.

39

Yeah, you were, said Toby. But that wasn't your fault. You were trying to help.

I remembered gripping his little arm and then even though I knew I'd saved him, had already pulled him back away from the danger of the water, I didn't let go. I kept holding him by his wrist, harder and harder. And then he screamed.

What happened then? said Toby.

I closed my eyes. The beer bottle was still in my had. Tight in a vice grip. I saw the boy's wrist in my hand. Tight in a vice grip.

I couldn't let go, I said.

I could see his face, he was terrified. He was screaming and the ducks must have been frightened by his screams because they were thrashing the water and flying out into the lake. Then there was a strong hand on my shoulder, pulling me back, someone shouting at me.

A man tried to make me stop, I said. But I couldn't. I mean I wanted to, I wasn't trying to hurt him.

I know you weren't.

But he said I was. He said get off my son. I couldn't. My hand wouldn't listen. It wouldn't let go and the more he shouted at me, the more I think I held it tighter. I knew I was hurting him, but I couldn't do anything to make it stop.

Then what happened?

I saw it clearly. I saw Dad running towards me, dropping to his knees, prising my fingers free of the boy so I screamed because he was hurting my fingers. Then Mum was there, crying, saying sorry to the man and the man's wife was there too, crying, scooping the little boy up, and then Dad and the man were pushing each other.

The dad said I was a monster, that I was trying to hurt his son, I said.

But you weren't, said Toby. You know you weren't. You were helping him.

I was, I mean I was trying to. But he kept saying he was going to call the police.

He did, said Toby. But your dad sorted it. No one thinks you're a monster, Roslin.

I nodded. I think I was crying. Suddenly, my hand released the beer bottle, and the bottle dropped to the rug, white froth foaming out on the grey carpet.

Toby jumped up and grabbed one of the throws from the couch, started dabbing at the beer. I just sat there. I felt even more like that runner, but I wasn't frozen. I was just numb. It was like the memory had wounded me, exhausted me, like bringing it back from wherever it had lost itself had wiped me out. I sat there watching Toby push the throw into the carpet, so it soaked up the beer. When he was done, he looked up at me.

I'm glad you remembered, he said.

I didn't answer. I was looking past him to the window. I saw nothing.

Roslin, he said, snapping his fingers. Come on, Roslin.

I blinked, my head jerked. It was like I was being pulled back into the now. I saw Toby clearly. There wasn't any worry in his eyes. They were blue and brilliant.

Enough moping, he said. I think me and you should get drunk. When does an uncle get the chance to lead his nephew astray. You up for it?

I nodded. Yeah, sounds good.

He stood up. I need more than that. Get your arse up, I need more than beer. Come on, we've polished off what your dad had, I'll drive us into Northwich, teach you how to really drink. Bourbon, that's what you need.

I copied him. Stood up. Tried to mirror his smile.

That's what I want to see, he said. Let's me and you open the gates and let the barbarians in.

I had this image then of barbarians flooding through a gate of some old city, like in Greece a thousand years ago, and the crazy thing is I wasn't sure if it was a memory, my own memory, or just a seed planted by Toby's words. I couldn't tell the difference. The barbarians raced through the gates, swords high, people screaming, and I didn't know if I was one of them or if I was the first poor nobody they hacked down or if I was just imagining Toby's words into reality.

# Six

We drank something called an Old Fashioned and Toby made a cocktail called a Paper Plane, but I couldn't drink that. He cooked us sea bass with fried potatoes but because he was drunk, he burnt the potatoes but, because we were both drunk, we ate them anyway.

Did I tell you about my book? he said, the strange orange cocktail swirling in Mum's martini glass as he leaned across the dining table.

We'd been smoking too, something I would never have dared to do in front of Mum and Dad even though I'm sure they knew I smoked. I suppose they were doing what all parents do, letting me make mistakes, but they never stopped me or judged me. I was kind of free in a way, but that freedom only stretched as far as smoking when they weren't there to see me.

You told me it wasn't poetry, I said. I was slurring my words. Not like before. This was just the drink. The good thing was, all the drinking had blocked off that horrible memory that I was wishing had stayed forgotten, and I was happy just to be sat with Toby like nothing else mattered but us drinking and eating.

He pounded a fist on the table dramatically. I'm done with poetry, he said. It's a bloody bourgeois pursuit anyway. A folly, Roslin. I've wasted years on that tripe. No one cares about poetry anymore. Do you know how many copies of *Savage Horizon* I sold this year?

I shook my head. I'd never read his books, never even read any poetry really.

A pitiful one thousand, he said, draining the remainder of his drink. That's it. How's a man meant to live on that? Well, I can't can I? I have to teach! Jesus! Do you know what that's like? Do you think Byron had to bloody teach? Do you think proper writers do? I'm done with teaching, the same as I'm done with poetry.

Maybe you should write a detective novel, I said.

He put down his martini glass so hard the glass clanked against the wood and for a moment toppled as if it might fall. Toby ran his hand down the stem and steadied the glass, swirled his head, yawned. Christ, no. I'm not a sell-out, Roslin. I'm writing a real novel. Do you want to know what it's called?

I took a sip of my bourbon. Even though I'd had four glasses, every sip still felt like bleach was being poured down my throat.

Is it called *I Hate Poetry So I'm Writing a Novel*?

He laughed. It was a roar, like I'd said the funniest thing he'd ever heard.

I should have called it that, he said, still laughing, glancing down the table for the bourbon, reaching for it, pouring a large measure into the martini glass. No, I'm not as clever as you. It's called *A Forest Anywhere*. Isn't that pompous? I know it is, you don't have to tell me. I'm a sell-out to the literati. It makes me sick.

I like it, I said. My eyes were blurry and when I moved it felt like too much of the world was moving with me. I took another drink, felt the burning liquid coat my throat, winced.

He slammed his fist on the table again. Me too, I love it. You know what it's about? It's about a kid your age who wants to get away from his life, but he can't. You know why?

I shook my head. I felt like if I spoke, I might burp and if I burped, I might vomit.

Because of class, Roslin. It's all class in the end, you'd

46

know that one day if you had the chance. I'm the working-class hero but you know what, I hate the working classes. I hate where I came from. But I'm a bastard, you know why? Because I use my socio-economic scars. You know how I got this book deal? I'll tell you. It wasn't because my poetry sales were so bloody good, it was because I went for dinner with a publisher and she asked me where I was from, so I told her. I said Toxteth. I said my dad was a boxer. I said my mum was a cleaner. I told her this beautifully false true story about how awful our life was, how little we had, and how much of a brute my dad was. Oh, she loved it. She loved that I was this working-class angel she could show off. It made me sick, Roslin. But did I say no when she offered me an advance? Did I hell. I lapped it up. I do interviews now, I was at a book festival last week doing one, and I tell everyone how important it is for working-class writers to have a voice. But I'll tell you the truth, my book isn't about class, that was a lie to tell you that. I hate lies, I do. It's not about class, it's about love, Roslin. That's what all good literature should be about, that's all that matters. Love is all you need. Love, love, love.

Toby trailed off into a stuttering song and then without warning he dropped his head to the table and gave a deep sigh into the wood.

Tired, he said, lips kissing the table. You're a good boy,

47

Roslin. You don't deserve any of this shit. You're good. Damn it, I love you.

Yeah, damn it, I said. I could have copied him. My head was that heavy. I wanted my bed, but I didn't like the idea of going upstairs. I was worried that if I stood up my legs wouldn't work properly, and I'd fall right back down.

You're a miracle, he slurred. A fucking miracle.

I brought my glass up to my lips to drink but the sudden waft of bourbon made my stomach retch, so I put it back down and took a deep breath.

Toby must have passed out. I could hear him snoring into the wood. I thought about shaking him awake, but instead I did something completely crazy.

I knew it was cold outside. It had been raining hard all night so a lot of the ice had melted or been washed away. The roads would be a slushy mess. When I was about nine, I went through this phase of taking off all my clothes and running outside so Mum and Dad had to chase me down the hill. I used to love that, me running down the street completely naked and them right behind me, laughing or shouting, embarrassed or full of love for their nutter son. I got that old thought in my head as Toby snored. It was nearly two in the morning so there'd be no one outside. I stood up, somehow didn't topple back down as I expected, and I took off my jumper, then my jeans, then my socks, until I was just in my boxer shorts. I chickened out of going all the way. Nearly naked was as good as naked, and anyway I only wanted to get outside and feel the night all over me. I don't know why but I had a sudden understanding that if I felt that sensation then I might forget all the other stuff. If I felt my body react to something, then it couldn't be messed up, could it? If I stood and the icy air traced itself all over my skin and I got goosebumps and I shivered and resisted going back in, forced myself to feel the winter on my body, then there was nothing wrong with that body was there?

I didn't give myself a chance to change my mind. I ran down the hall, opened the front door and jumped outside onto the pavement. I felt the freezing air hit me immediately and it felt wonderful. It whacked me in the chest, took my breath away, and I loved it. I did a kind of star jump. When I landed there was a bit of ice left on the pavement, so I slipped a little but caught myself on the door frame, managed not to fall. I spread my arms wide and made a kind of woohoo call that I knew was ridiculous but when I did it, I felt like an animal. I was a wolf howling to the moon except the moon wasn't there because there were clouds hiding the moon. I shouted out again. A cat screamed back at me, but apart from that there was no other sound. No one turned on their lights or opened their curtains to bang at me to go inside. No one called the police. No one saw me.

But I saw something. I was looking up into the clouds. The moon's light was there, a smudgy glare behind the grey. I knew it wanted to come out, to be freed, and so I was about to call to it again, but then I saw the hawk.

I'd never seen a hawk over the village before. There are loads out over the fields and I even saw one as we were driving to Delamere once. It was just sat in the road pecking at a small rabbit. Dad had to slow the car, beep at it to move, and even then, it tilted its head to us as if annoyed before flying off. But this hawk was further up High Street at the top of the hill over the graveyard. It was hovering, or at least I thought it was hovering. The more I looked at it, a black arrowhead against the dull clouds, the moon's light pushing through to shine on its wings, the more I could see that it wasn't moving at all. It was still, completely still, not circling, not riding the air. And what was it doing here in the night? It would be blind, unable to find any prey. Out of place, wrong and stuck in one fixed point. I watched the hawk, kept waiting for it to move on a flow of air, but it was motionless, frozen, yet it didn't fall from the sky to the road, didn't tumble to earth. I kept watching, hoping I was wrong. Hoping it wasn't frozen. Not like the runner.

I don't know how long I stood there, watching the hawk, but eventually I had to accept that it was unmoving. Utterly, completely. It was still and wouldn't deviate from that stillness. I became still too. I couldn't feel the cold anymore. I didn't even register that I was virtually naked. How much time passed? The night remained the same. The moon stayed behind the clouds. There was a silence that stretched and stretched. I'd like to think it was only minutes, that I stared at the hawk for a few minutes at most. But I know it wasn't. I know hours passed. I know morning crept closer. I know the darkness changed. I know I was captivated.

A glare of light broke that captivation. A car horn beeping forced me back to the awareness that I was now standing in my doorway, near naked. I felt the exposure to the night air then, felt how it was in almost every part of my body, felt my teeth chattering as they must have been chattering all the time I was stood there, felt that my fingers and toes were numb and my hands at my side were shaking uncontrollably.

I didn't look to see who was in the car. No one drove through the village at that time unless they lived in the village, and anyway, they probably already knew me as the weird Roslin kid. I came back inside, slammed the door. I had to grip the banister as I climbed the stairs because my whole body was shivering. I went straight into the bathroom and turned on the shower, danced up and down on the cold tiles as I waited for steam to fill the bathroom. When I could feel the heat of the water pulse against my body, I stepped into the cubicle, my boxers on, and I let the burning water, hotter than the bourbon even, cover my whole body and wash the ice away. I let it pour over me until my body had stopped shivering and my teeth were calm and I could feel my fingers and toes, and then I stayed there longer, closed my eyes, pushed my head against the shower wall. I saw the hawk. I saw it as if it were out there in the fast-approaching morning. Waiting, unmoving because that lack of movement was its instrument of patience. Waiting, fixed in one point but not frozen. I saw its body flicker as if released from the watching, knowing there was nothing down there to dive upon. I saw the hawk turn and circle on the air to ride the morning out over the graveyard and above the church as a hawk should.

# Seven

On Tuesday, we drove to Liverpool.

Do you know what I love about this car? said Toby.

It's fast, I said.

Truth is, I don't have a clue about cars. I can drive because Dad taught me when I was about fourteen, but I don't exactly enjoy driving and I've never taken my test even though legally I can now.

Toby accelerated. The road was empty. We were speeding past Runcorn, but it seemed there was no one else in the world. Just us two and the Jensen. It was almost eerie, like there was some kind of lockdown we hadn't been told about. Everywhere felt absent, missing. The only thing that seemed active was a wind that was blowing hard up from the river.

Toby switched the radio from Radio 6 to Rock FM.

Harry Styles came on so he switched channels to Radio 2. Sam Fender came on and Toby let that play.

Nah, Roslin, he said. What I love about this car is that it was free. Did I ever tell you that?

I looked out of the window. The car was low to the road. A white van came up on my side, the wind buffeted the van as it came too close to the Jensen, but Toby accelerated again, and we quickly outpaced it.

I don't think so, I said, glancing back at the white van. I could see the driver eating a pork pie.

I used to date this girl called Fiorella, he said. This was her car. She was Ecuadorian and rich. It was years ago, back when I was at uni in Durham. Anyway, we split up. She cheated on me if you want to know, some posh prick on the rowing team. We didn't speak for months, but when we graduated, and she was going off to New York for an internship at some fashion house, she turned up at my flat and just handed me the keys. I was hungover. Maybe I was a bit cruel because I didn't let her in. I think maybe she expected that we'd sleep together. She said something about loving me, but all I could see was this baby parked out front and I kept thinking, wow, that's mine now. I think she tried to kiss me. I pulled away. I know, I'm heartless. But the gist of the story is that this was her car, and she gave it to me just like that. For a couple of years after I kept thinking she'd come back for it, but she never did.

He tapped at the steering wheel.

That's a very romantic story, I said.

Toby laughed. And what would you know about romance? You've hardly lived.

I know enough.

I'm sure you do, Roslin. I'm sure you'd surprise us all with your tales of heartbreak and desire, so shall we just say I believe every word?

I shrugged, laid my hand against the thin glass of the window. The glass was cold, a whistle of air sneaking through a gap and kissing my forehead.

We crossed the new bridge. The Mersey was at low tide. The mudflats looked like little islands. I swear I saw a man walking between the islands, but the sun was low and too bright, blinding as we sped over the bridge. The rungs of the supports were slats cutting up the dazzling sunlight. It's like a ship that bridge. Every time I go over it, I imagine it's like this BBC series I watched, *The Terror*, where these ships get stuck in the ice in Canada, trapped there as the weather gets worse and worse. The rungs of the bridge kind of undulate too. As you drive across, you watch the first set extend up and up, and another set of rungs come down the other side.

They're like sails but the bridge, like those ships, can't go anywhere.

Toby talked about the last time he came to Liverpool as we drove through Speke then Aigburth. He got a little sentimental as we approached Toxteth. Pointed out his old school, the shop where he used to buy a Snickers and Cherry Lucozade every morning, the church his mum and dad got married in, the graveyard his nan was buried in, the house his first girlfriend lived in. By the time we turned off a main road and were heading through the backstreets past a park, I swear he was about to cry. When we finally got to Cawdor Street, I could have cried with him.

Welcome home, he said, not to me but to the memory he'd wanted to find waiting for him that had died with the truth of what had become of Cawdor Street.

He parked the Jensen and neither of us said a word.

I hadn't been to Toxteth for years. When I was little, Mum used to drive up to see an Aunty Kate who lived somewhere near Cawdor Street. She drove me down her old street but never stopped. She never even said much. No reminiscing. No anecdotes. No family secrets. It was only Dad who told me about Cawdor Street, how Mum had grown up there, how tough it had been with how Mum's dad was. It's bad, I know, I was more interested in my terrible grandad than anything else. His name was Christos but apparently everyone called him Christy. I knew he was a boxer; I'd seen a photograph of him once in baggy shorts and heavy gloves, about to jab towards the camera. He looked hard, nasty. He must have been about six-foot-eight, massive. But it was Dad not Mum who told me he'd been in films in the sixties, had even gone down to London at one point. That's where Mum's older brother Giannis was born though I've never met Giannis. Dad didn't know much about the films, what specific ones Christy was in, but I think some were Hammer Horror and he was definitely in a war film with John Wayne. Just as an extra, nothing major. I know it's stupid, but I was more interested in Christy than I was with Mum's childhood, more interested in knowing about his life even though I knew what a bastard he was. Maybe that made me a bit of a bastard too. You shouldn't get drawn to bad people, should you? It's like serial-killer documentaries on Netflix, I know there are people who love them but every time I try to watch one, I just think about the lives those people took, how evil they were, and I can't keep watching. Reality can be sick sometimes; I'd rather imagine a reality than know one. Maybe that was why I liked Christy, because of how Mum and Toby felt about him, how much they wanted to wipe him from their lives; he was just a half-drawn life, and I had to imagine the rest of him.

What have they done to the place? said Toby.

The house we'd parked outside was boarded up, as were the houses either side of it. I looked across the street. It was the same story there. Boarded up everywhere and then occasionally, weirdly, one or two houses that looked lived in with nice curtains or a newly painted front door or an electric car charging out the front.

Maybe they're going to knock them all down, I said. Which did you and Mum live in?

Toby slumped back in his seat.

Surely, they wouldn't, he said and then this big sigh. Surely.

We sat there for a while as Toby just stared at the houses. I didn't know what to say. He was grieving, maybe that was what was going on. This was his childhood wasn't it, these houses and this road. And now here we were watching the corpses of that childhood, but they'd been dug up and put on display. I just let him have his moment. The radio was still playing but it wasn't any kind of music that fitted the mood. It was something crazily upbeat by Lizzo that I don't think was exactly Toby's taste. We sat there looking at the broken windows and graffitied boards. After a few minutes, Toby shook his head. When the song ended, he started the engine and we drove off without another word. I could tell he wanted to get out of there as quickly as possible, but the street was full of speedbumps so we had to go achingly slow. I looked at the houses, tried to imagine Mum in one of them, little-girl Mum, but they all looked too empty to ever have contained a life let alone the lives of whole families.

We drove into the town centre and parked in the Q Park.

Are you hungry? Toby asked.

I wasn't. I'm never hungry anymore. I eat but if someone asks me, like Toby did, if I'm hungry, I have to lie because people expect you to need food.

I could eat, I said.

There was an Italian round here somewhere, he said, scanning the street as we came up out of Liverpool One. He didn't look like he knew where he was. We stood on the curve of a road as taxis and buses streamed by. There was no absence in Liverpool, the city was full of shoppers and as we stood waiting to cross, we were surrounded by people waiting to do the same.

An old woman carrying too many bags got up really close to me, but I didn't have any room to steal some space from anywhere. Shoulder to shoulder with strangers, the feeling of bodies behind me, this intense pressure to move, to not be still.

The lights changed. As we crossed, Toby was scanning the streets with a frown.

Maybe it was up there, he said, pointing down a narrow side street.

There's a Subway, I said. I could eat Subway.

Jesus, Roslin, we're not savages. Come on, I'll find us somewhere.

We kept walking, pulled along by a flow of people until they went their own way, and we were crossing towards a large mock-Tudor building that said Rigby's on it.

There? I said, more hopeful than anything.

I'm not saying I hate cities because I don't. I love going shopping in Liverpool and I even loved the Tube when we went to London last Christmas, but it only takes me about half an hour of being in a city to start feeling enclosed. It's not like you can just turn down a street and be in a field surrounded by no one. It's not like you have that easy get-out. It's just building, building, building. Street, street, street. Cars everywhere and too many people to lie to yourself that you're different. Maybe that's it, maybe a city just makes me remember that individuality is a myth.

It'll do, said Toby, though I could tell from his voice it wouldn't do.

We were about the only customers in the pub, but we sat in the back room where there was a real fire. We ordered sandwiches that weren't awful. When we'd eaten, Toby started getting excited because he realised we were close to the Cavern.

You have to love The Beatles, he said as he drained the last of his half of porter. It's your heritage. It's in your blood, Roslin. Sing me a Beatles song, go on, any song.

No way, I said. I'm not singing in a pub.

He spread his arms. He'd cheered up now, no more maudlin grieving over a dead street or a changed city. Come on, he said. Don't be scared of being seen. I'll start.

He stood up. There was no one else in the room and the bar was hidden round a corner, but I swear as he started singing 'Here Comes the Sun', I shrank right into my chair.

Little darlin', he sang and to be honest he didn't have a bad voice. It's been a long, cold, lonely winter. Come on, Roslin, get up.

The pub was near silent. Just the faint mumble of horse racing on a television in the snug.

Toby grabbed my arm and pulled me up.

Sometimes, he said, you just have to forget about the world and sing.

I don't know the words, I said.

He laughed. What's that mother of yours been teaching you all these years? Here comes the sun, do da do da, just hum it if you don't know the words. Come on. Here comes the sun.

I started singing very quietly. Here comes the sun, do da do da.

That's it, Leo. Louder.

He started shouting the words.

The barman appeared, watched Toby singing like a drunk, shook his head and vanished back to the bar.

I love this city, said Toby. You know in London I'd be chucked out for this. Come on, one last burst. We'll sing it together because we can.

And we did. We stood in that pub and sang that stupid song about the sun on what must have been one of the coldest days of the year, and even though I didn't know a single word I copied Toby until we were both shouting *It's alright, It's alright.*

Yes, Roslin, he shouted, and he fist-pumped me like he used to when I was ten. That's what I want. I want to see you live. Did you feel that?

He pulled me into a hug and, almost the same as Dad, he suddenly went very quiet and just held me. It was awkward but no more awkward than singing in a pub in the middle of the afternoon, so I let him hug me.

Remember, he said, his voice just a whisper. Remember to live. Do you hear me?

I nodded.

No, I want to hear you say it. Say you want to live.

It was just a song, I said, and I tried to pull away, but he held me harder, closer.

Just say it, Roslin. Say it.

Okay, okay, I said. It felt like he was going to crush me. I want to live, okay.

Yes, he said. So do I. There's nothing else is there? We just need to live. We just need to forget the rest and live.

When he finally let me go, I would have been ready to get back in the Jensen and drive home, but instead we paid, Toby singing 'Here Comes the Sun' as we left, and we went straight to the Cavern.

You know this isn't the real Cavern, said Toby as we descended beneath the city into a bleak damp darkness. There were posters on the walls of bands I'd never heard of. I knew about the Cavern, I think Mum might have brought us there once. I have this dim memory of sitting somewhere that smelt like the river or a sewer while an awful band played. It was busy, full of tourists, but I remember Mum and Dad dancing. I think that's the only time I've ever seen them dance.

There was a band playing as Toby ordered us a drink at the bar. I'm not tall but I had to duck as my head was touching the glistening vaulted ceiling. My shoes were sticking to the floor as I walked.

Toby handed me a pint of Guinness.

I used to come here every Saturday when I was your age, he said as we sat at a table.

There was a table of Germans in Liverpool shirts next to us.

Toby sipped his beer as the band sang. They were a Beatles tribute band, but they weren't singing 'Here Comes the Sun'. They were singing a song I knew, one Mum used to play. She'd even sing it to me sometimes. 'I've Just Seen a Face'. I like that song, it reminds me of being a kid and not understanding anything, you know like when you see something or hear something and you don't have to understand it, you just exist in it, absorb it. I think all childhood is like that. You just absorb things until eventually you do understand them and they're kind of ruined then. Not this song. It wasn't ruined. Even though they weren't the real Beatles, they weren't wrecking the song.

Yeah, every Saturday, said Toby. Me, Tooley and Spencer. We used to sit right here probably, listen to shit bands, drink beer that was a pound a pint, and chat up Swedish girls. It was glorious.

I nodded. I was sort of rocking to the singing. *Fallin', yes I am fallin', and she keeps callin' me back again.* The words sounded so innocent, childish even. I don't know why, but my mind flashed back to the girl in the church. I hadn't seen her face yet, not properly, but as the fake Beatles sang a love song, it was her that leapt into my head. I'm not crazy, I'm not saying I loved her. I didn't even know her, but she was there, leaning against that old oak door, looking pretty lost and apart from anyone else. *I've just seen a face, I can't forget the time or place.* But we hadn't met, and she wasn't the girl for me, she was just a memory I'd stumbled on at that moment.

Toby was talking but the music was loud, and the small space had quickly filled up with more tourists, so I could hardly hear him. I nodded every now and then, sipped my Guinness, and watched the band. The more I watched the band, the more I started to think about what a strange thing a tribute band is. There were these four men, all of them in their late forties, dressed like The Beatles from years ago, those same collarless suits, all of them with the same haircut though these must have been wigs, moving like The Beatles must have moved, kind of bobbing to the song. But they weren't The Beatles. The Beatles don't exist anymore. Most of them are dead and the version of The Beatles they were copying wasn't even the only version of The Beatles. I've seen them in photographs. The Beatles had loads of different styles, yet these false Beatles had focused on one style, copied that. Somehow that's enough to say to the audience that they are The Beatles, to ask them to suspend their collective disbelief and invest in the lie that these four men are The Beatles. But they're not. This John Lennon was definitely Indian for a start. This Paul McCartney was too short and too fat. I'm not entirely sure what George Harrison looked like close up, but I could see whisps of blond hair beneath this George Harrison's wig. This Ringo Starr was too far back in the dark of the little cave stage they were playing in, so I couldn't make him out, but the indisputable fact is he wasn't the real Ringo Starr. They were all just copies, not even exact copies, and they were getting away with being copies because maybe people needed them to exist as copies. I glanced to the Germans. They were all singing. I saw Toby looking even happier than he'd been in the pub. I saw people dancing all around me even though it was barely three in the afternoon. They were all fine with the lie. They didn't care. I think they even wanted the lie. But for some reason, I felt angry at the idea that we were all being lied to. I almost wanted to stand up and shout that these weren't the real Beatles, that they were a fraud and that they were all being stupid pretending to believe these Beatles were even half as good as the real ones. I know that was irrational. I knew it as I was feeling it, but the more they played and no matter how well they played, the more I hated them for being a lie. I can't explain it in any other way. I hated the fact that they weren't the real Beatles, and we were all pretending that was okay.

I didn't say a word. I drank my Guinness, and we stayed in the Cavern for an hour. When we were driving home, it was snowing. Night had fallen far too quickly. As we drove back over the new bridge, I didn't once think of it as a ship. It was a bridge, and we were crossing it to go home, that was all. Just because something looks like a ship doesn't mean you should tell yourself it could be a ship.

Toby was in a good mood. Lewis Capaldi came on the radio, and even though I'm pretty sure that's not his type of music, he turned it up loud and tried to sing along.

As the Jensen rolled slowly up the sludge-riven street

towards my house, Toby asked me the exact same question Dad asked me a week earlier.

What do you want to be, Roslin? he asked as he parked.

The snow had turned to rain and the road was a grey mess of sludge, tire tracks making dirty black streaks.

Did Dad tell you to ask me that?

No, I was just curious. Why, has he been pestering you too?

Not quite. It was just last week he came into my room. Mum had gone really upset at dinner, just started crying like she does, and when she went to bed, he came in and asked me that.

And what did you say?

I said I want to make films.

Direct?

I nodded. Yeah, maybe. Or maybe just write screenplays.

That's ambitious. I like it.

But it's a lie, I said.

The truth was I had to tell Dad something. He seemed so happy when I told him that my dream was to make films. I couldn't hurt him by telling him the truth, I couldn't do that.

What do you mean a lie?

Toby had turned the Jensen's engine off and the car was getting cold quickly. I shivered but he didn't seem to take the hint.

I mean it's a lie, I said. I was sure Toby wouldn't be hurt like Dad might have been. There was no reason to keep lying.

In what way though, Roslin? Come on, help me out.

I shook my head. It was so difficult to put into words even though the truth was as simple as any truth could be. It was just that saying it seemed hopeless even to me and I was the one thinking it day in day out.

It's a lie because I can't see the future, I said.

Toby laughed. Of course, you can't, mate. Nobody bloody can. No one is expecting you to do that.

I know, I know. But I don't mean I can't see it like I'm looking in a crystal ball or something. I mean I can't see it like it's just not there. No matter how hard I think about it and how much I know I'd love to make films, I have this deep and complete feeling that there isn't a future. It's like if you said to me would I like to meet for a coffee tomorrow and I knew there wasn't going to be a tomorrow, I'd have to say no because I couldn't meet you, could I? So, when Dad asked me, just like when you asked me, I knew what I should say because I really want that, but if I'd said the truth, I would have said I can't be anything because I can't see myself having a future.

I expected Toby to tell me not to think like that or to say something generic like, don't worry, all teenagers feel that way, but he didn't say anything. He just sat there and looked at me. When he eventually did speak, he didn't say any of the things he should have said.

I understand, he said. I wish that wasn't the case. But I understand.

Do you? I said. I wasn't looking at him. I was looking ahead, up the hill to the church. There was no one there. Snow lay white upon the stone wall that enclosed the graveyard and upon the church roof and tower. There was no girl. No hawk.

I do, said Toby.

I believed him. Toby saying that seemed to open this gate in my mind and through it came something that I'd never told anyone. He listened as I told him. He didn't stop me or tell me I was wrong or tell me it was silly or just my imagination. He listened and through that listening I felt like everything I'd been thinking for months now was real and not crazy and above all, that it was okay for me to have those thoughts because they were my thoughts.

I told him this. I told him that it wasn't only the future

I couldn't see. I told him that when I try to think of my childhood, I can see most of my life but if I try to think of what it was like being four or younger, I just hit this black wall. I'm not saying I struggle to remember anything from my childhood, I get it, I know most people don't really remember being very young. What I mean is that when I try to think of being that young, I hit this impenetrable black wall and it's almost a physical thing, right there ahead of me, over me, solid. It's like I walk right into it, and it says no, you can't go any further, and I get this sick feeling, like real nausea, and unless I stop thinking about being very young that nausea stays, and I feel like the black wall is all around me. So, I don't think about being young, ever. I just shut that off. I told Toby that. About the wall and the sick feeling and he listened. He sat in the Jensen and let me speak. When I was done, he said we should go inside and have a cup of tea and watch a film. He didn't say anything about what I'd told him. Eventually, he got out of the Jensen, waited for me to follow him, and put his arm around me.

Come on, Roslin, he said. Let's get you inside.

# Eight

The next day, we stayed in and watched old films. *Hud, The Apartment, If, Watership Down, Don't Look Now.* We watched *Lucky Jim* too, the 1957 version. I'll admit it's pretty of its time, and I don't exactly agree with the representation of women as objects of desire, but I love the last scene where Jim is completely drunk on stage giving this lecture about Merrie England. I like it when Jim says that even the idea of this idyllic past of dancing round maypoles was all phoney baloney, that it never was merrie, that it was murder and there was starvation and tyranny and all that. I like that honesty, even though he's obviously very drunk when he's being honest and for pretty much the entire film he hasn't been honest, he's been too timid and submissive, but I don't mind that it's the drink that makes Jim suddenly tell the truth, or his truth at least. Everyone has a trigger, don't they? Everyone has something that pushes them over the edge, not into madness or violence, just into that chasm of truth we all probably need to fall into at some point if we want to be real. I think that's why I like *Lucky Jim*. It's all about truth and that's something I think about a lot. My truth, what that is and how I find it.

I think Toby likes *Lucky Jim* because it was a book too and maybe because he thinks he's like Jim. I know he says he hates being working class, but Jim is kind of a working-class archetype battling against middle-class archetypes. I bet that's how Toby really sees himself when he's down in London. This kid from Liverpool writing poems and beating them all at their own game, a game he didn't even know the rules of before he started playing. It's harsh, but he reminds me more of this character called Bertrand. Bertrand is the snooty professor's son, he's this avant-garde, jazzy snob who looks down on Jim, but in the end, Jim steals his girlfriend from him. Bertrand is very sleezy. I'm not saying Toby is that sleezy, but he always seems to go through girlfriends who are always a bit younger than him and even though they're usually writers or artists too, none of them are ever as successful as he is. I'd never tell Toby I thought he was like Bertrand. I think that would hurt his feelings too much, and anyway it does no harm him thinking he's like Jim.

We ended up watching *Die Hard* because it was nearly Christmas. Just as it all kicks off with the terrorists, Toby started yawning.

I think that's me done, he said, standing up, arching his back, yawning again. You carrying on?

I was laid out on the couch under this thick fleecy blanket.

I might just fall asleep here, I said, though in the back of my mind I was thinking of doing a *Die Hard* marathon, or at least the first three films.

Don't stay up all night, he said though there was no conviction in that parental advice.

He yawned again and mid yawn he theatrically slapped himself on his head. I knew there was something I meant to give you, he said. It's just come back to me.

He tossed me the remote and hurried out to the hall. When he came back, he had a book in his hand.

I'm not a massive reader. My mum will tell anyone that. Ever since I was little, Toby has been trying his best to get me reading, Dad too in his way. Dad is really into Jack Reacher books. I did try reading them at least. I think I got through about three, but the truth is I'm more into films. To me a film is a kind of book. It's a narrative after all, and when I watch a film, I'm reading it too. I'm reading how it's shot, the acting, the lighting, the setting, the dialogue. I'm reading with just as much focus as Toby reads his poetry or Mum reads her Kazuo Ishiguro books about talking dolls or whatever they're about.

Toby placed the book on top of the blanket almost apologetically. He hadn't stopped trying to get me to read but I suppose he must have started to feel it was a losing battle.

Now listen, he said. I'm not expecting you to read this. Me giving you this isn't about you reading it.

I sat up, picked up the book.

Isn't that what giving someone a book is always about? Reading it?

Don't be a smart arse, he said.

I looked at the cover. There was nothing on it except for the author's name and the title. It was a very light blue that seemed almost green in the faint glow of the paused television. David Jones. *The Anathemata*, I said.

Well done, said Toby. The title's the trickiest part.

But I'm not meant to read the rest? I said.

I turned the book over. No blurb. No synopsis. No clues. I opened the first page. On the inside jacket there was an endorsement by WH Auden.

*Very probably the finest long poem written in English this century*, I read.

I know, I know, said Toby. Sounds scintillating. But listen, that book means a lot to me. I first read it when I was about your age, maybe a little older, and I didn't understand a word of it. I spent years thinking that's what I needed to do, understand it. I read it over and over, and you know what, I did understand it in the end. I got the references, the intertextuality, the subtext, all of it. I got it because I love poetry and words, but then I kept reading it and you know what happened?

You got an Audible account instead?

He gave my head a light swat. No, Roslin. I started to not care about understanding it. I started to accept that understanding it was in a way killing the pleasure of it for me. I started reading lines out of the context of the rest of the poem, just opening the book at any page and reading a few words. Loving those words for what they meant to me on that day. I know poetry will never be your thing, but I thought maybe that you having something and understanding you didn't need to find answers in it, no matter how complex and puzzling it seemed at first, might help you. In the end, it's all just a bunch of words and there's a crazy beauty in that. I don't care if you don't read it all, but maybe there's a few words in there that might speak to you right now. They might be just what you need even though you don't know you need it. You're a puzzle, Roslin. You always have been. A beautiful, unsolvable, amazing puzzle, so why not see that there are other puzzles out there and not all of them are better for being solved.

He rustled my hair. Night, Leo.

I mumbled night back. I was flicking through the first pages. Pages and pages of a preface. I've no idea what a preface is. I heard Toby going slowly upstairs, heard his bedroom door shut, heard his feet on the carpet and then his bed creak as he got in. Finally, I came to a page with white space.

I, Rite and Fore-Time, I read.

I yawned, reached for the remote to press play on *Die Hard* and flicked the page at the same time. I pressed play and as the racket of American voices filled the room, a few words on the page caught my eye. I didn't speak them, just mouthed them.

*as in the young-time, in the sap-years:*
*between the living floriations*
*under the leaping arches.*

I have no answer for what happened next. It was like the words were a trigger to send me into an instantaneous dream. I don't even remember shutting my eyes. Wherever I was, where the words had taken me, I wasn't in the living room. There was no *Die Hard*, no noise at all. I was walking in a huge hall. It was cold in the same way a cathedral is cold. Every Christmas we used to go to Liverpool Cathedral for this carol service. I always remember Mum used to make me wear about three jumpers and a thick coat on top, but it still felt cold in the cathedral. Not deep-in-your-bones cold, it was more like the place was so big, so immense and open, that I felt like I was outside even though I knew I was inside. Wherever I was felt that same way. I have no idea what floriations means but all around me there were these wide pillars towering up and all over them were flowers, but the thing was all the flowers were grey. In fact, the whole place was grey. I peered up into the darkness and could just make out that the pillars were holding up arches, hundreds and hundreds of arches that were so far apart they might as well have been leaping to each other.

I was walking. I've had loads of dreams, most in the past year had been really vivid and intense, but as I walked in this dream, I didn't feel confused like I did usually. I knew I was going somewhere. I knew my walking had a purpose. After a few minutes, I realised my feet were bare and that there were pools of water on the floor. That didn't stop me walking. I didn't mind my feet getting wet even though the water was ice cold. What was strange was the sound that echoed out into the vaulted space as my feet slapped against the pools. It was like clapping. It echoed and the echoes dispersed only to be followed by more clapping as my feet touched water again.

When I saw the boy, I knew who he was.

It was the pyjamas that made me recognise him. Paw Patrol. Mum has them still in a box in the attic along with the rest of my baby clothes and all the teddies I can't remember the names of anymore.

Hello, I said.

I stopped.

The boy was standing in a pool of water. Everything fell into quiet. My voice didn't even echo.

The boy was about five. His hair was long, nearly down to his shoulders. I touched my own hair which was short but the same brown.

Who are you? asked the boy but I think he knew the answer. I think maybe he was a bit scared and that's why he asked it.

I think I'm you, I said, trying to keep my voice soft, kind.

Oh, he said. I thought so. That means you're Leo too?

Yes, and you're Leo too.

He smiled. I'm Leo too.

Where are you? I asked.

I'm here, he said.

Where did you come from? I asked.

He frowned so hard it was almost a scowl. Where did you come from? he asked.

Here, I said. I've always been here.

The younger me shook his head. No, you haven't. I've always been here. I was here first. I'm me.

And I'm me too, I said. I was here before you.

He shook his head again. No, I'm me and you're you.

There was no point arguing with a five-year-old.

Where's your mummy? I asked.

Younger me looked back into the darkness. There was nothing that way, not even the vaulted arches and immeasurable columns.

She's all the way back there, he said, pointing into the dark.

He turned back to me. He smiled and his hand went into the pocket of his pants. I used to keep Kinder bars in those pockets and forget about them so when Mum did the washing, she'd be pulling out wrappers and squashed chocolate from the washing machine.

I watched as he brought his hand back out and held it towards me. His little fist was closed.

She asked me to give you this, he said. He opened his palm.

I stepped closer until we were no more than an arm's length apart. In his hand he was holding a seed like a pumpkin seed.

What do I do with it? I asked.

I don't know, he said. She said it's not mine anymore, that if I was a good boy, I had to give it you.

He pushed his hand towards me. I could see reluctance on his face. He didn't want to give the seed to me. It was his, that's what he knew and that's what I think I knew too. But I took it anyway.

When the seed was in my hand, I closed my fist around it. I'm not a kid, I don't mind sharing, but right then and there I didn't want anyone else to have that seed, not younger me or anyone, so I hid it in my fist so that nobody could take it.

I saw sadness on the face of younger me as he watched my fist enclose the seed.

I need to go now, he said.

Where to?

Here, he said, and he pointed to the ground. I need to just stay here.

Oh. Where should I go?

Younger me pointed past me into the grey space of columns and colourless flowers.

You have to stay there, he said. You need to turn around.

It was like he was commanding me, but as soon as he spoke, I knew he was right so I turned around.

Ahead of me I could see a soft glow, a humming light. At first, I thought it was the television but then I saw that within the light there was a small speck of black. Slowly, the black started to grow, spread, and it grew and grew, aching closer to me, until there was no light, no grey, no flowers, no columns, no leaping arches. I stood there, my seed hidden within my fist, and I let the black sweep over me.

Are you still there? I said to younger me.

There was no answer.

I'm here, I said.

# Nine

I think you can outwalk a dream. I know that sounds like nonsense, but to me a dream isn't a physical entity, I know that, but they do happen in physical spaces. Usually two physical spaces. One, the human who is dreaming the dream, their brain which is within their body and maybe, if you want to get spiritual, their soul or just their consciousness which is creating the dream. Two, the space in which the dream is happening, the place where your body is when you're dreaming. That's usually a bedroom or wherever you've fallen asleep, although I have a theory that most people have their real dreams, the most vivid and impactful ones, when they're in the familiar setting of their bedrooms. It makes sense that to forget about a dream or push it away, you have to create distance between one of those physical spaces and yourself. You can't distance yourself from your body unless you're on some kind of transcendental plane that I don't believe exists, so the only way you can really ever forget about a dream is by outwalking it, by getting as far as you can away from the space where it happened or the scene of the crime. You could even try outrunning the dream if you could, but I'm not much of a runner so I just outwalked this one.

Before Uncle Toby was awake, I took myself away to somewhere separate from the space where I dreamt to one I knew was real. I think another essential component of escaping dreams is to be somewhere you can feel reality to the point you could touch something and say I know that's real. The only time I feel like that is when I'm walking in the fields around the village.

As soon as I stepped outside my house, I knew that I wasn't going to go near the mere. The runner was a dream, he must have been. I kept telling myself that. The runner was a dream. A kind of waking dream. Maybe I'd zoned out as I was walking that day, or maybe the cold sent me into some kind of trance. He wasn't real. The hawk wasn't real. The younger me and the seed he gave me definitely weren't real. But I couldn't chance going back to the exact spot where that dream had happened in case I dreamt the runner again and started believing that he was actually real.

I walked down through Great Budworth, turned right towards Comberbach. It was even colder, and I'd forgotten my hat so by the time I got to the bottom of High Street, my ears were burning cold. Most of the pavement was slick with an icy sheen that even my walking boots were struggling to find a grip on, so I had to keep stepping out in the road where there were still little ridges of soft sludge that hadn't frozen.

As I came out into the dell at the bottom of the village, I heard a bird calling in the trees. It was silly but I got a little bit shaky. I'm not exactly sure what sound a hawk makes, they always seem so silent, and if I think about it, they probably shriek, scream almost, but this sound was more of a morning song, yet I still imagined there was a hawk above me and if I looked up I'd see it there, hovering without moving. I kept walking. There were so few other sounds and hardly any cars on the road.

When the road rose out of the hollow, I saw the sun was low on the horizon again but today it wasn't fiery red, it was almost white like a negative disc drained of warmth. I kept walking, aware that with each step I was walking further away from my bedroom, further away from the runner. As I walked my body adjusted to the cold, so I hardly felt it by the time I got to the Cock O'Budworth. My legs were moving, my body was awake, my mind focused only on the act of walking and moving and moving. The more I walked the more the dream seemed to fall away from me, bit by bit like crumbs. I hoped I wouldn't find those crumbs on my way home like Hansel and Gretel. I'd find a different way back and leave the crumbs of that dream to be pecked at by magpies. Let those birds dream.

I thought about turning right after the Cock, up past the private school, because I knew there was a footpath I could take back to the village but it seemed too soon to go back that way. Even though I was wide awake, far from dreaming, I put my head down and marched on past the school, walking hard, my feet stomping at the pavement, breaking ice. I could have run then. I know I said I'm not a runner, but I had this crazy thought that maybe I should have started running. That maybe if I was the runner, I'd never see that other runner. Be the runner, outrun the runner. But I didn't run, I just got into this very purposeful striding until I was nearly at Comberbach. I felt like a rambler.

There was a field on my left and a little brook wriggling across it, so I came off the road and followed the water. I'm not sure if it was someone's field or whether I was allowed to walk on it, but it was so early I was sure no one would be about to tell me I was trespassing, and anyway that striding was carrying me forward. I'm not saying I was running away like I was scared, but there was something unstoppable about my walk that morning, like I knew that I'd only stop walking when there was nothing left to walk away from. And I wouldn't know when that was, only my body would, and my legs would slow, and I'd breathe and find a wall to sit on and stop.

I was lost in the act of walking, so I didn't even see the runner until the sound of a car whizzing down Gibb Hill made me look up. The sun was even whiter. The sky was clear and white too. Sunlight danced on the brittle needles of ice-grass. I froze.

I knew it wasn't *the* runner within a second. It was a woman, maybe in her forties, but it wasn't just the fact this runner was a woman that told me she wasn't my runner. She was actually running, moving. I stood there, suddenly feeling how cold my ears were again, snuffling, breathing hard from the exertion of the walk. The runner was heading out towards the road. She was moving fast. She had a snood pulled up, covering most of her face. She was wearing all black apart from a bright orange headband. Her ponytail bobbed as she ran. She looked like a runner. Her legs kicked back in a smooth, professional rhythm, and her movement was constant. I watched her until she was on the road. She turned right, kept moving with that steady, easy pace until I couldn't see her anymore.

I wasn't scared. My heart wasn't racing. But I didn't move on straight away. I know that seeing the woman meant nothing, that she wasn't my runner, but in the moment of seeing her form, I felt like I was falling off a ledge. Like a dream-slip, that sense of falling where you catch yourself and it takes a few seconds before you realise you aren't falling, that you're safe.

I patted my gloved hands together as if that clapping would pull me back to my senses. My clap was answered by a bark.

Over the far side of the field, past the brook towards Budworth Lane, there was a little Patterdale barking towards me. The first thing I thought of was this news story on Yahoo about a man who cloned his pet Patterdale. They can do that now. When you know the pet you've loved and cared for is nearly ready to go over to the other side you just snip off a bit of their fur and spend about fifty thousand pounds to send it to a lab in Zurich or Geneva, somewhere like that, and a year later you get an exact clone of your dog. The crazy thing is you can even specify the age. You can say I loved Buddy best when he was three, so they send you a three-year-old Buddy. I wonder sometimes if that new Buddy has old

Buddy's memories. He must, mustn't he? Surely for Buddy to love his new owner as a full-grown three-year-old dog he needs to retain some memory of that love, otherwise what kind of a relationship would that be? They'd be strangers to each other. It might be a clone of Buddy but without Buddy's memories it wouldn't be Buddy and it never would be. It would be a different dog. The owner might as well have gone to the RSPCA and paid £100 for a stray. I mean they might end up loving each other, new Buddy might end up being the best dog ever but that new Buddy, no matter how much of a good dog he was, would never be the Buddy the owner thought they were getting would it. If you ask me, I think that kind of thing is wrong. I think if you have a pet and love them you shouldn't want to replace that love in exactly the same way or share it with a dog that isn't technically your old dog. That doesn't seem fair on the first dog, to miss out on all that new love. I get how hard it is losing something you love but really I think you should try to make a new love with something or someone new, not just copy it like love as if our connections between each other are so tangible we can expect them to be transferable. Real love isn't transferrable, is it? It's dependent on the specifics of the relationship. The who, when, why. You shouldn't believe you can keep making copies of love forever. Let it go, remember it, love it all the more for that memory. That's my philosophy anyway. I'd never clone my dog.

But this Patterdale wasn't Buddy. Buddy was in Australia, and this Patterdale was stood in a field in Cheshire. Behind him I saw a man coming up from the road. The man stopped, tapped his leg, and the Patterdale stopped barking and sat. The man was wearing a flat cap and a coat that looked like it might be a football coat, maybe Man Utd from the black and red. I couldn't see much of his face except he had a thick black beard. I stood there watching him and he watched me. Maybe I should have waved or made some gesture to show this wasn't strange, we were just two people walking in the morning, but the way he stood there with arms folded across his chest, studying me almost, didn't seem right. He'd come from the same direction as the woman. I don't know if it was the way he was dressed, like a scruffy game warden or something, and I know it was unfair of me to think, but I had this image of him following the woman, like those foxhounds following the scent of a vixen. I didn't like that, and I didn't want to wave to him. I know it was morning and winter and too early but as soon as I saw him there was a kind of heavy emptiness on the air that made me feel suddenly far away from anyone.

Eventually, he gave a sharp whistle through his teeth

and the Patterdale jumped up and ran back down the field towards Budworth Lane. The man gave a slight nod in my direction, unfolded his arms, and turned to follow the dog.

I didn't hang around the field but nor did I go straight home. Like I said, I wasn't in charge that day of when the walk was done, and even though the man had made the morning feel eerie and dangerous, I didn't turn right when I left the field and came on to Gibb Hill. I kept walking left, down into Comberbach. I took my phone out as I walked. It was nearly eight o'clock. As I walked through the village, I passed people scraping ice from the windscreens of their cars, kids in school uniforms waiting at the bus stop outside the Spinner and Bergamot. Everything was waking, life was creeping into the frozen morning, but I had nothing to do but walk.

Sometimes when I walk, I get into this zone where I'm switched off from the world around me because I've hooked in to one thought or memory. It takes a while to get there but by the time I'd crossed onto Budworth Lane and was starting the long walk back home, I was in that zone. There was nothing else. I couldn't hear the cars, my own breathing, the low waking moans of cows, the lonely solo song of a robin. What I was lost in that day was Christmas. It wasn't that many days away, and I think I must have started mulling over what I would get Mum and Dad, but then I must have thought back to what I got them last year. It was there I found the hole. No matter how hard I tried to remember, I couldn't find anything. No image of wrapping Japanese whisky for Dad or an expensive candle for Mum. Nothing. And then I tried to remember what they'd got me, like that would fill in the gap, that I might see myself unwrapping their gifts to me and in doing that find a way back to the memory of what I'd given them. But again nothing. I went back to the year before. Nothing. I went back year after year. Nothing. Nothing. Nothing. I knew what I had in my bedroom. I knew there was a PlayStation 5 and some Marvel Funko Pops on my shelf, and a dartboard I never used hanging on the back of my door and a boardgame called Hero Quest that Dad loved from when he was kid, but I'd never opened, but I didn't have a single memory of receiving any of those as Christmas presents. That can't be normal, can it? I knew it couldn't. I felt like I was falling again as I reached the village, but this time it wasn't a little fall. I felt like I had only been falling forever, free-falling into a black sky. I was almost scraping inside myself, pulling apart the room of my memories for that one glimpse of me sitting in the living room on Christmas morning, excitedly tearing wrapping from a present and seeing what was inside. But there was nothing.

I was so lost in that desperate need to remember, that I walked right past my house. It was only when I was standing outside the church that I realised I'd gone too far. My legs were done, burning like my ears. I was at that point where my body had decided the walk was over, but I felt worse than when I'd left. Instead of a dream that was haunting me I had this impossible-to-ignore thought that there was something wrong with me. I was seventeen, not seventy. There shouldn't have been so many chasms in my memory. I hadn't lived long enough to be so full of them that I had to clear the old ones out like I was a cheap laptop. I could handle not remembering being a baby or a toddler, but surely I should have been able to remember a Christmas present from a year ago.

I was staring into the graveyard, past the graves like the memory was out there somewhere, when the door to the church opened and the girl with red hair came out.

# Ten

I'm not some Casanova, I don't go round talking to girls just because I think they're pretty or that I'd have a chance of them liking me. I'm not saying I'm an introvert or too tongue-tied to even talk, I just never seem to get the opportunity and anyway, it's a little creepy isn't it, thinking that a girl would want you to talk to them just because you want to talk to them. I suppose that if I think about it, that was what made seeing her feel so unique, almost meant to be. I'm not a romantic either. I don't believe in love at first sight and I'm not crazy enough to say that was what I felt. It was simpler than that. I just wanted to know her. Since seeing her that night, I'd found I couldn't stop thinking about her. Thinking about what her name was and why I'd never seen her before and why she was standing there that night outside the church singing. Maybe that was why I went up to her that morning even though it wasn't something I'd ever done before. Or maybe Toby was right. Maybe I'd never looked for that sort of thing before and then there it was looking right at me, right in my village, so there was no excuse not to talk to her was there?

Even though I only had a minute to think about it, I planned out exactly what I was going to say as I walked up the path to the church. She saw me, tilted her head, frowned a little. It was okay, I was going to ask a question about the church, so she didn't think I was walking up the path solely to talk to her and then I was going to side-step into asking her about herself, just sound casually interested. But I didn't get a chance to say any of that.

I saw you, she said, when I was still a few steps away. She wasn't frowning now. She was smiling but in a knowing way. Yeah, you were watching me the other day. That was you, wasn't it?

I couldn't ask anything about the church now. I couldn't side-step into anything.

What? I said. I wasn't watching you; I just saw you.

Yeah, you were, she said. It's okay. I was watching you too. That's what people do isn't it? Watch each other.

She leaned into the arched stone of the doorway, relaxed, like the church was her church.

Unless you're a weirdo, she said, still smiling. Are you a weirdo?

I'm not a weirdo, at least I don't think I am, but when you're asked something like that it's almost an impossible question to answer truthfully.

It's okay, I like weirdos sometimes, she said, before I could speak. She spoke fast, excited. She was well-spoken, a kind of theatrical posh voice.

I'm a weirdo then, I said.

She did something odd then. She looked me up and down, almost like she was scanning me, assessing me, and her head did that little tilt again. She nodded.

Yeah, you are, she said. What's your name weirdo?

Leo, I said.

Rah, she said, laughing at her own roar. Are you a Leo too? I'm an Aries so I'm a fiery mess. What are Leos?

I'm not a Leo, I said. I'm a Sagittarius.

She shrugged. I don't really believe in star signs to be honest. It's like churches and religion. It's all magic, isn't it?

I looked up at the church. I think I believe in God sometimes, mostly at Christmas when we go to a carol service or at Grandad's funeral when I really needed to believe in God, but I think on the whole if I was honest, I'd say I was an atheist. There can't be a God can there because then we'd all have to accept that we were someone else's idea. I want to be my own idea.

Yeah, I said. It's all crap.

She did this over-the-top hurt face and stood up straighter like she was shocked. That's not very nice, she said. I'll have you know I'm a good Christian girl. My dad's the vicar here? Didn't you know that?

She did the head tilt.

Sorry, I didn't mean to…

She laughed. Don't be silly. Do I look like I'm stupid? Of course there's no God, just don't tell my dad I said that. Where do you live anyway? I don't think I know you and I know absolutely everyone round here.

I glanced back down the hill and pointed to our house. Just there, the house with the white door.

She stood on tiptoes and narrowed her eyes. That house? I didn't even know it had been for sale.

It hasn't, I said.

So, when did you move in?

When I was two, I said.

She shook her head. It was an over-the-top shake. No, no, no, she said. That's not right. I've lived here since I was ten and I've never seen you.

Well, I've always lived here. How old are you?

She bit her lip. How old are you? Are you like twenty?

No, I'm seventeen. I mean I'm eighteen soon.

She wrinkled her nose like a rabbit. I'd never seen someone so expressive with their face. It seemed like every thought that went on inside her head came out in her face, in how she raised an eyebrow or pushed out her lip or tilted her head.

That's not old, she said. I'm sixteen.

What's your name? I said.

She looked up, bit her lip again. It was as if she were trying to make up a name.

Hmmm, she said, looking back at me. I'm Eadie. I know, it's ugly but it was my gran's name so you can't be mean about it.

It was cold and standing there so still as I talked to her made it seem even colder. I don't know how she wasn't freezing. I was wrapped up in a jumper and my heavy coat, but she only had on her school blazer. Her cheeks were red, though she wasn't shivering, didn't even seem bothered by how cold it was.

Do you go to Belmont? I said.

She looked down at her blazer as if she'd just remembered she was dressed for school.

Sometimes, she said. Not today.

Oh, I said. Why's that?

She tilted her head again, scanned me.

Can I trust you, Leo?

I folded my arms over my chest. I've only just met you, I said.

I know that. But trust isn't about how long you've known someone is it? Trust is about that person's character, who they are inside and what they believe in. Do you believe in trust?

I tilted my head. She raised her eyebrow at that, but I didn't mind. I've never really flirted with anyone, but it felt like that moment of copying her tilt was a kind of flirtation. She was pretty, I liked how fast she talked and how she seemed so full of her own energy that even the cold wasn't pulling her down like it was dragging at me.

I believe in trust, I said.

Good, me too. I can trust you then?

You can, I said. As long as I can trust you.

I think I'll let you, for now. But this isn't about you, it's about me. It's a very sad story.

Your story?

She shook her head. No, not my story. I'm never sad. But you're probably wondering why I'm not in school. You probably think I don't care about my education, don't you?

I thought maybe you were ill, I said.

No way, she said. I never get sad, and I never get ill. I'm choosing to be off because of the sad story. Do you want to hear it?

I nodded.

Good, it makes it almost less sad when I tell it to someone, she said. She was talking faster now, not slouching in the doorway. She'd even moved a few steps closer to me, away from the door, as she spoke.

Go on then, I said, and I did something really brave then. I took a step closer to her. She did this little double take, just slight, but already I could tell that kind of thing was for effect with her. She didn't step back.

I like face-to-face stories, she said. Okay, prepare yourself. I used to have a sister, Leo. That's really sad isn't it. Used to. Don't look so sad though, your face doesn't suit sad. I used to have a sister but that doesn't mean she's dead or anything, or at least everyone thinks she isn't dead. Her name was Becca and she was nineteen. She got the normal name. Rebecca Sproston. I know, my surname is almost as ugly as my first name, but Becca is a nice name, and my sister is lovely. Was lovely. See that's why I'm not in school today. Oh my God, you would have loved my sister. She was fun and funny, she was too confident and too old for her own good. She loved

100

bees too. I never thought anyone could love bees like she did. I used to call her Becca Bee, that's how much she loved bees. Every item of jewellery she owned had to be a bee. She had bee necklaces and earrings, bee rings and bracelets. She used to have this jewellery stand in her room and even that was shaped like a bee. Anyway, today is like an anniversary of when my sister went from *is* to *was*. It was this exact day four years ago that she vanished. Just like that, puff, like magic. One day there was a Becca and I loved her, and she loved me, and then there wasn't a Becca.

Where did she go? I said.

She crossed her arms. I couldn't help wondering if she was copying me.

Shush, Leo, she said. This is my story. Anyway, that's the exact reason why I'm not in school today. Where did she go? That's all I ever ask. Where did my big sister go? You might think that being the kids of a vicar we'd be perfect children, good as gold. I am, I think, but Becca wasn't really. She never liked doing what Dad told her to. She was only just nineteen when she vanished but she'd been doing what she wanted for years, going out and not coming home for days. I suppose in a way she'd vanished before, but she'd always come back. This time, precisely on this day four years ago, she vanished and never ever came back. You'd think the police would investigate like it was a crime wouldn't you, but the thing is my sister told us all she was going to vanish. She stood in our living room on this morning four years ago and told my Dad she hated him, that she never wanted to see him or us again, that she was going to go away and none of us would ever see her again. Isn't that horrible? It's not sad, is it? It's mean. I was twelve but she didn't even care how upset I was, she just walked right past me while I was crying and when I ran to the door to pull her back, she pushed me off her and told me to go away. That's cruel too, isn't it? I'll never forgive her for that, but Leo, I still love her, and do you know what else, do you know why I'm off today? I mean I'm not just sad and need some time to grieve or something. Do you know why I'm really off and I think I might be off more until I don't feel this way anymore?

No, I said. My arms had relaxed. I'd been watching as she spoke. Her voice going faster and faster. And there in the corner of her eye was a single tear that stayed there, trapped in her eye, refusing to drop. What do you feel?

She let out a sigh. I feel like this, she said. I feel like my sister didn't vanish. I feel like something terrible happened to her. I feel like it's up to me to find something so everyone can stop pretending that she vanished and find out what happened to her.

What do you think happened to her? I asked.

She took a deep breath. I don't know if it was the first time she'd ever said the words, but it felt like she was building herself up to admitting something she'd never admitted before.

I think, she said, slow, not racing. I think somebody hurt her. Not somebody, this one person. I even know his name. Prendergast. Isn't that a horrible name? He doesn't even live too far from here. That makes me feel so sick, that he's out there, living while she's dead. Because I really believe she's dead, Leo. I know she's dead, I can feel it in my bones, and I think I have to help her by finding out what happened to her, by finding out what he did to her and where she is. Do you believe me?

I think I do, I said, because she'd said it so seriously, with so much truth, that my immediate thought was yes, you're right, I believe you, so I didn't know what else to say.

You really believe me? she said.

No, I said. I mean, yes, I believe you. If that's what you think, then I believe you.

She smiled. I knew you weren't a weirdo, Leo, she said. I knew I could trust you when I saw you staring at me.

I wasn't staring at you, I said.

You were, she said. But that's okay. I'm giving you

permission for that now, just that once. If you stare at me again, I'll think you're a pervert or something. I trust you, though. I knew I could.

I've never asked a girl out. That's pathetic, isn't it? I was seventeen, nearly eighteen, and I've never been on a date or kissed a girl or done anything with a girl ever. I know I shouldn't have felt it because of how sad her story was, but if I was in some trashy romance story, I think I would have kissed her then. Or at least I wanted to kiss her. I know, you can't just kiss someone like that, it doesn't happen that way, but we were standing so close together and there was an undeniable tension between us buzzing with energy. She was looking at me and we were smiling at each other.

I didn't kiss her, of course I didn't.

Maybe I can help you, I said.

She tilted her head. Help me? What do you mean?

I shrugged, shuffled back away from her. I mean maybe we could meet up and I could help you.

She grinned. Wow, she said. You are a weirdo aren't you. Are you asking me on a date to look for evidence that my sister was murdered?

No, I said. Like that the buzzing energy burst. I knew I'd ruined any chance of anything between us. I just meant that I could help, I said.

She did something I didn't expect then. She touched my arm. It was gentle, a calming touch that said don't worry, I was joking.

I knew what you meant, she said, her hand moving away. Maybe you could. How about we make a deal. How about if you find anything that you think is a clue to what really happened to my sister then you can bring it to me. I live just there.

She pointed to the house on the other side of the graveyard.

How am I meant to know if it's a clue? I said.

She grinned. No idea. How am *I* meant to know? Have you ever heard of kismet?

I shook my head.

It means something is meant to be. Fate, Leo. So, if we're meant to meet again then we will, and the way fate will show itself will be through you finding something that helps me. That sounds horribly selfish, doesn't it? Oh well, I'm fine with that. I mean, we've lived in the same village all our lives, if you're telling the truth, and we've never seen each other until the other day. Either we were never meant to meet, or we were only ever meant to meet today. So why not leave the rest to kismet. Do you agree?

I nodded. I hated the idea of kismet, fate, all of that. It

felt too close to a kind of God, someone out there deciding something on my behalf. But she'd said the word and I think I was already lost in the palm of her hands even then.

Kismet, I said.

She smiled, stepped back towards the church door. When she was at the door, she tilted her head again.

Kismet, she said, before pushing the door open with her shoulder and quickly slipping inside.

# *Eleven*

I woke up to the sound of Toby whispering on the phone. He'd been sleeping in the spare room which was next to mine. I glanced at my phone. It was only six in the morning, but I could definitely hear him talking to someone in a low, almost conspiratorial murmur. I didn't catch all the conversation but as I lay in bed listening, I realised it must have been Mum he was talking to.

Even though Dad had promised to let me know when they'd got to their resort safely, I hadn't heard a word from them. I know how that could seem strange to an outsider, but I was happy with the sense of isolation and independence that disconnect had brought me. I felt older, freer, more myself than I'd ever been, so even though I'd typed a message out to them both, even though I'd been right on the verge of ringing them a few times, I didn't do any of that. They were in Bermuda. That was all the story I needed. And I was at home. They must have known I was safe, trusted me even. That felt good, to believe that the reason they hadn't called was because they trusted my maturity and capability to care for myself. I was nearly eighteen after all, isn't that what was expected of eighteen-year-olds? Yet there was also this nagging question that wouldn't stop bothering me. Why hadn't they called? Was there another reason I wasn't aware of? Had I done something wrong, something terrible? Surely it wasn't the thing at Marbury, that was months ago. Had they really been storing up their hate for me for that long and then just decided to abandon me? No, that didn't make sense, but then that left the question existing without an answer and the more it existed without an answer, even though I was convincing myself the answer was that this was all okay, the more the question refused to budge so it grew and became less a nagging annoyance and more a weight that couldn't be ignored. Why hadn't they called? What had I done?

I asked that question as I lay in bed listening to Toby. Mum had called him, or he had called her, at six in the morning. That was a crazy time to ring someone. At first, I thought maybe something bad had happened. As I listened, I tried to catch evidence of that. Toby saying something about hospitals, asking how Dad was, asking how it happened, whether they needed anything. But there was none of that. No matter how hard I tried, I could only catch a few words and phrases.

*More time. Are you sure? He's fine, but listen, no just listen, please. I'm not saying that. I know, it was hard, I know. But Soph, don't you think. I know, you're right. I'm just worried. I was wrong. Needs you. Okay, stay there. I promise, he'll be fine. Trust me, Soph. Of course not, I'll call you as soon as. He'll be okay, he has me.*

I closed my eyes as I listened to Toby's fragments. It was clear who he was talking about. Me. Maybe Mum missed me. Maybe I missed her. It was too early to be awake, and the room was dark and all the world outside as quiet as night. Toby's words faded. I must have drifted into sleep.

I hate dreams. They're all lies aren't they. No matter how real you think they are when you have them, they're not real, they're just your thoughts and memories and needs all jumbled together into a false narrative of images and imagined moments. I hate dreams because the ones I have are always so vivid and invested in the attempt to convince me they're real. I know I can't say what other people's dreams are like, I only know what dreams might be like from films and television shows and that's all a lie too isn't it, another

109

imagining, but if I think about my own dreams then what I know for sure is that in the last year especially they've been getting more vivid, more intense, more convincing in that façade of reality. I've really struggled pushing them away, outrunning them, outwalking them. Sometimes a dream will stay with me for days, weeks even. I can see it every time I close my eyes like it's a memory, something that actually happened, and even though I know what I'm remembering is only a dream I have these moments of doubt where I question whether a dream is really just a dream. I do things like tell myself that a dream happens in the mind and so it contains a kind of reality. We see everything with our minds, don't we? Our eyes see things and our brains connect the dots so that we're aware and conscious of what we're seeing. The brain is the mind so everything we experience is in a way just the same as a dream. I tell myself that the only difference with a dream is that they happen unbidden. We are unconscious when they begin, and we stay unconscious throughout the dream. Waking ends them because when we make our eyes open our mind has to process what we're seeing and the dream can't exist in tandem with that. I tell myself that, and I convince myself sometimes that the dreams are so intense because they're real. That's an easy path to madness, I know. It doesn't last, my rational brain kicks in and I fight off that urge to believe in the lie. I run away from the dream even though I'm no runner, or I push it away as best I can.

The dream that came to me after listening to Toby was part old dream and part new. I knew that straight away. My unconscious self said, wait, I've seen this before, when the old dream kicked in, but it was the new dream that began the dream.

Of course, it was about Eadie and of course it was about kissing her.

We were in her room. I have no idea what her room was like, so I think I just imagined a generic girl's room, pieced together from my only real source of knowledge of what a girl's room might be like, television and film. She had a white four-poster bed. Not like a medieval bed, more Ikea than Gothic. Her room had a beach feel about it, the floorboards a light wood, the wardrobes and units the same white as the bed. Her bedsheets were white too and her pillows a light blue. There was a dreamcatcher on the wall and one of those letter signs that light up attached to the wall behind her bed. It said DREAM, but I think that was only because this was a dream. I don't think Eadie would have something like that in her room.

We were on her bed. Things were getting urgent. Our

mouths were urgent. Her hand was on my chest. I had a shirt on, but she'd unbuttoned it. My hand was on her bare thigh. I felt like I knew we were going to have sex but then we stopped kissing.

What did you say? I said, because I knew I'd heard someone speak.

Nothing, she said, kissing me.

I pulled away. Her hand stayed on my chest.

You did, I said.

She smiled. You're just nervous.

We kissed and then I couldn't feel her lips. I think it was because I'd stopped thinking about feeling her lips, her body, my need for her at that exact moment, and started to think about the voice I'd heard.

The voice was from an old dream and so when I began to think about it and stopped feeling Eadie's kiss, I knew I was in the old dream.

I thought, hello, I know this place because I did know it.

I was running beside a river. I knew what river it was. It was the River Weaver, and I was down beneath the Blue Bridge near Davenham. I think I must have been about five because I ran with that crazy freedom you have when you're a kid that age, when the act of running is a game in itself even if you aren't being chased. I don't know if this was an exact memory because it didn't feel completely right. I know that Mum and Dad would take me for walks down by the Blue Bridge a lot when I was younger, but as I was running, I became aware that it was Mum who was running after me, and that clarity of knowledge was what felt wrong. If this was a memory then I knew, though I couldn't pinpoint the exact memory, that it shouldn't have been Mum chasing me.

She was calling something. There was panic in her voice though I didn't hear her words. I was too happy running. The river was to my right. There were moorhens and I was running towards them, clapping, happy, unstoppable.

Then I came to a cliff. This is another reason why I hate dreams. It's stupid how they shift about so wildly and without any rational sense of reason or purpose. I hate that in films too, cut-jumps that take you away from the central narrative and only serve to confuse. In all my favourite films I like linearity. A straight line. Beginning, middle, end. There's a film called *Memento*. I hate that film. It's about a man whose memory is all jumbled. I think that film is told in reverse, I don't know for sure because every time I've tried to watch it, I've got so annoyed that things weren't moving forwards towards an end point that I've switched it off. I believe that all the best stories gain the trust of the audience or the reader or whoever through simplicity. Here's what's happening, come with me and I'll tell you straight how things are resolved. Don't pull away from the central story, don't mess up my understanding by trying to be clever with the structure. That's what my dream did, and I hated it even more for doing that.

There was no river, no moorhens, no Mum chasing me.

I was standing on a cliff. I've never been to a cliff in my life. I've seen the White Cliffs of Dover loads on television and I know what a cliff looks like and I can imagine how it must feel to stand on the edge and look down at the sea or rocks. That's what I did. Five-year-old me looked down from the cliff into water. I knew I was going to fall. It wasn't fear or that split-second moment of knowing something bad is going to happen when you can't do anything about it. I wasn't afraid of the space below me or the possibility of falling. I didn't try to step back or cling to something. I simply knew I was going to fall and there was nothing that could be done to stop that. Not kismet or fate, just reality. The fall had already happened and would always happen. Over and over and over. There was nothing I could do to prevent myself falling, so I gave in to that inevitability and stared down into the vast chasm of space and the slow undulation of water below. The water was calm, only small waves that made nothing but a half attempt to rise, more

114

like a river than an ocean. There were no rocks. Just blue water. It was so clear that water.

I think that's why I could see myself in the water. I'm not saying I saw a reflection of myself from that high up. That would be ridiculous. It was more an image of myself and for some reason I was more aware of it than actually seeing it. It was like a phantom that was both in the water and in my mind.

The me I saw was five like the me watching. I was wearing the snowsuit I knew I was wearing as I stood on the cliff edge. My arms were outstretched as if I were crying for someone to pick me up, but I wasn't crying. My eyes were open, but I knew the image of me in the water wasn't seeing anything. Vacant, those eyes saw absolutely nothing.

What I saw from the cliff edge was a body floating in calm water.

I was dead and I knew there was nothing I could do to save myself from that ending. Linear, ongoing, inescapable, repeating, bound by the happening. I would always be that child in the water, and I would always be the child watching myself in the water.

I'm not kidding, I hate dreams.

# Twelve

E uphemia arrived that same day.

One of the first things she said to me was, *If you dare call me Euphemia once I'll make you into a terribly horrid character in my next book. I will, I'm very cruel like that.*

I swore I wouldn't. I would have sworn I'd do anything if she asked me. I've never seen a woman as beautiful as Euphemia Allam. That's probably not the best way to feel about your uncle's girlfriend, but to be fair I didn't even know he had a girlfriend before Euphemia knocked at my front door. My very first thought was that she looked out of time. I don't mean she looked in a rush, I mean she looked like she didn't belong in the now. She looked like she was from the 1920s, I suppose even her name seemed to have been plucked from another time.

As soon as I opened the door, she gracefully barged in past

me and dropped her bag on the carpet. There was a scent I couldn't name but I knew it must be the scent of expensive perfume. I saw a film once set in Paris about a writer who could travel to the Paris of the 20s. Euphemia could have been stepping through time as soon as she stepped through my door.

Where's that bastard poet? she said. Even a swear word sounded soft from her lips.

I was staring at her; I know I was. Her brown hair had these perfect crinkles in it and was cut short so her long neck was exposed. Even though it was snowing again outside, a biting wind blowing in after her, she wasn't wearing a coat. She was wearing an oversized jumper with a long, pleated skirt underneath, a small clutch purse in her hand. She leaned against the staircase and opened the purse and took out a small silver cigarette case. She opened the case and inside was a row of different-coloured cigarettes.

Do you mind, Leo? she said.

I shook my head.

She was watching me watch her.

I know you're Leo, she said. Your uncle showed me enough photographs. You'd think you were his. God forbid that's true. Can you imagine? Incest in the suburbs and all that. Not quite the suburbs I suppose, working-class incest.

Oh, Toby would love that. I shan't be surprised if that's not his next novel.

Probably, I said because I couldn't think of anything else to say.

She smiled, took out a duck-egg-blue cigarette and, putting the cigarette case away, she took out a lighter, lit the cigarette and took a deep drag. When she blew out the smoke, her lips pouted into a heart. I think I might be romanticising the memory of that moment, but I don't think I care. Euphemia, Em, was so beautiful she might as well have stepped out of a romance novel into my hallway that day.

I must say, she said. You're a damned sight more handsome in person. Quite the Tom Holland look to you. I like it.

She smiled again. I realised then she wasn't much older than me. Was that hope? I wasn't standing there planning on seducing my uncle's girlfriend, but I think I was annoyed that Toby, enough years past thirty to be done with women in their twenties, was dating someone who, if I had an ounce of charm or confidence in my body, I might have felt I had a chance with.

Come on then Spiderman, she said, taking another drag. Let's go wake up the Poet. I drove past a delightful-looking pub just up the road there. It's after twelve, I'd say we all need some lunch even if that lunch is a solely liquid affair, don't you?

I did but I didn't say I did. Pub, I said. He's in bed still.

She laughed at that. Can't have a pub in bed, can we? No, that won't do. Why don't you be an utter darling and wake him up for me while I get changed. She pointed to the living room. I'll go in there so don't go barging in on me. You wouldn't do that would you, Spiderman?

I shook my head. She took another drag of the cigarette. I watched the white tip touch her lips and the fire flare at the lit end. I wanted to be that cigarette.

Good chap, she said. She picked up her bag and went into the living room, cigarette between her lips.

Toby told me all about Em as he dressed.

Euphemia has potential, he said as he put on a black shirt. I don't mean as a girlfriend. Don't get me wrong, Roslin, she's an incredible woman but I'm not picking out rings any time soon. Don't judge me, we're on the same page. If I'm honest, our relationship consists of reading each other's writing more than anything else.

I was standing in the bedroom door. I must have been frowning because he grinned as he sprayed some aftershave on his face and roughly smacked his cheeks.

Don't look at me like that, he said.

She's not far off my age, I said.

He grinned again. She's twenty-six you twerp. And before you ask, no, she's not nor has she ever been my student. We share an agent that's all, met at an awards evening in September. She's an astounding talent. Have you ever read any Ali Smith?

I shook my head. She's posh, I said.

Of course, she's bloody posh, said Toby. Her dad is some kind of baronet or something. Christ, imagine he knew a scally Scouser was shagging his daughter. I'd probably be dragged to the House of Lords, hung, drawn, and quartered. Anyway, you should read some Ali Smith. Em has more than a hint of her about her, though nowhere near the finished article mind. She's raw, hasn't even written a novel yet.

So, you're what, her mentor? I said.

I knew he must have heard the jealousy in my voice, I was barely hiding it. Don't get me wrong, my Uncle Toby is a very handsome man, and I can completely understand why someone like Em was attracted to him but it was like I'd seen the possibility of something I never thought was possible only to find out that he not only already knew it was possible, but he'd experienced that possibility. I think I hated my uncle that day.

It didn't get any better in the pub.

Em sat on my side of the table so that our legs were touching. Toby was oblivious. He spent the first hour in the pub talking about how many words he'd written of his novel since he last saw her. I've never seen anyone listen and get away with looking so disinterested as Em did. She couldn't have made it any clearer that she was bored by what he was saying, but she kept listening, nodding, smiling, and Toby didn't seem to have any idea he was boring the socks off her.

That all sounds completely marvellous, she said. She was leaning forward a little on the table and as she did her elbow touched against my hand. I haven't written a word in a month, she said. I'm a very bad writer, I know it.

Toby took a drink of his lager. Not bad, he said. Just disengaged. I told you, you need to throw yourself at the thing.

Is that what you told me to throw myself at? she said.

Probably not the only thing, said Toby. But listen, you just need to step away from everything else, give yourself to the book for a month or two. That's what I do, it's the only way. Full immersion.

Em yawned. It wasn't a rude yawn. I don't think Toby even registered it. She sat up, her leg still touching mine.

Leo, she said. Do you hate books? Please tell me you do. Tell me you love football or something.

I'd drank my first beer fast enough to settle some of my nerves so I could actually speak to her by my second. The pub wasn't busy. We were sat at a table on the bar side, a middle-aged couple on the other table and a man in high vis sat at the bar talking to the landlord.

Yeah, I really hate books, I said, and she laughed.

For God's sake, Roslin, said Toby. How did your mother raise such a philistine? Do you know how many books I've given him for Christmas and birthdays?

Too many I should think, she said. She wasn't looking at Toby. She was leaning into me, chin rested on her hands. I've never been looked at by anyone with such an intense interest. I would have loved that look to have been a different kind of interest, but the truth is it was more like she was looking at something she'd never seen before, something strange and new. I wasn't either of those things. I was just a seventeen-year-old boy.

Em, said Toby and his voice seemed to snap her back to the pub.

We both looked at Toby. He didn't look angry but for a moment I saw this glimpse of concern on his face. I didn't know who he was worried for, me or Em.

Em's leg moved away from mine. the little barb of tension that had stabbed into the air was plucked away.

Beautiful Leo, she said. Are you going to shatter all my illusions? Do you love football and *Fortnite*? Are you that kind of brute?

He's not that much of a philistine, said Toby. Go on, tell her what you want to be.

Even though she'd sat back, she was still studying me though with less intensity, a sort of hidden study. I was okay with that. I liked her studying me.

Go on, she said. Tell me. I'm all ears.

She picked up her wine and sipped it.

I don't really want to be anything, I said.

Toby tutted.

You absolute brute, she said.

He's a bloody liar, said Toby. Tell her, don't make poor Em think I'm from a family of no-marks.

Don't be mean, Toby, she said, though she didn't look at him. I don't think she'd looked at him all afternoon.

I'm not being mean, he said, taking another, longer drink of his beer. I just want him to show himself a little.

Okay, I said, but only because I wanted Em not to think of me as a no-mark, wanted her to see that I wasn't just some kid into *Fortnite* and aimlessness. I like films, I said.

Likes them, said Toby, almost jumping forward in his seat. You're an auteur, a protégé. Do you know he makes his own films?

Em took another sip of wine and gave a slow nod. I like films, she said. When I was your age, I used to imagine I could be an actress but then I moved to London and realised I wasn't pretty enough.

That's rubbish, I said before I even knew I'd said it.

Toby laughed. Suave, Roslin, he said.

I just meant she could have been an actress, I said, but they were both laughing now.

I felt suddenly very much like that kid I didn't want her to think I was.

I could see you in films, I said, trying desperately to pull her back into her study of me. I think you could have been in a Godard, something New Wave.

Oh, she said, and her leg touched against mine again. I like New Wave. My mother looks like Jean Seberg. Did you know that, Toby?

She turned to Toby.

He doesn't want to meet my family, Leo, she said, but she wasn't looking at me, she was still looking at Toby.

Toby threw his head back in exaggeration. Not this again, Em, he said. What are you trying to make us? Am

I meant to stay at the family pile one weekend and show them all how your bit of rough isn't so rough after all? Do you need Daddy's stamp of approval before I propose to you with your Nanna's ring?

No, Toby, she said. Maybe I rather hoped they'd like you that's all.

He laughed. It wasn't Toby's usual open, kind laugh. There was an edge of bitterness to it that didn't suit him. I felt suddenly like I was in a domestic argument, and I was very aware of my leg touching Em's. I felt like an adulterer, like I was betraying my uncle just in touch. I moved my leg away.

I'm sure they would, he said. I'll amaze them by reading Petrarch in the drawing room after sherry has been served. Your papa can tell me what a sport I am for trying to be like them and when we make love, I can call you Your Ladyship. It'll be very Lady Chatterley. You'll love it, I'm sure.

He seemed very proud of that last reference. He took a satisfied drink of his beer, draining the last of it, then put the glass down slowly on the table.

Em copied him. She placed her wine glass very carefully down, all the time smiling.

You can be an absolute prick at times, Toby, she said, very

steadily and without any emotion. I'm not quite sure why I came all this way.

He laughed. It was a scoff this time. I didn't like this version of my uncle; it wasn't one I'd ever seen.

We both know why you came up, he said. I never should have told you.

I think the argument would have continued but at that moment the pub door opened, and a young couple came in carrying a beagle puppy. Em jumped up and started stroking and fussing over the puppy, asking its name, how old it was. Toby went to the bar and ordered more drinks.

When the couple had gone to their table, Em sat next to me as we waited for Toby to be served.

I'm sorry about all that, she said.

I'm sorry my uncle was so mean, I said.

She put her hand on mine. Not holding it, just touching it as she'd touched my leg with hers. Her touch was light, but it made me feel heavy, fixed in place.

I'm glad I came, she said. I got to meet you at least.

Before I could say anything, Toby came back from the bar with a tray of drinks.

Right, let's put the aside this silliness and have some fun, he said. I've asked for a table; dinner is on me. The landlord is chilling the champagne as we speak.

Sounds splendid, I'm famished, said Em, and I was surprised that the two of them could change so quickly. There was no flatness in her voice, just what seemed an honest and excited response to my uncle's suggestion. And Toby was smiling as Toby usually smiled, no bitterness, no bubbling tension. Just Toby.

We ate dinner and we drank champagne. We drank too much and Toby told a story about a famous writer who he saw cheating on his wife, and Em bettered it by telling us about the time she slept with a famous married actor and only found out he was married the next week when she met him and his wife at her niece's christening. They told story after story about life in London, the parties they went to, the people they met. All of Toby's stories were tinged with an almost Marxist judgement of the crowds he mixed with while Em's were full of joy and wonder at the madness of that world. By the time last orders were called we were all drunk.

As we were leaving, I noticed that there was a Patterdale sat at the bar. I was much drunker than I'd thought I was, and Em was having to help me put on my coat. The world shifted and ebbed. The Patterdale lifted its head and looked at me. I swayed, looked up at the man sat next to the dog. I saw a thick black beard, but the man didn't look at me. Em tugged on my arm. Toby pushed the door open. Icy night swept in. We walked arm in arm down the icy pavement, Toby leaning against houses to get his balance, almost pulling the three of us over, we laughed and laughed, and when we were home Toby fell flat on the sofa and Em collapsed next to him. Everything was moving in a way I didn't want it to. I looked at Toby, his arm over Em's back. Their bodies seemed to fit together even in the small space of the sofa, and even though I was drunk I was angry at myself for what I'd been feeling since Em first appeared at the door. I was a terrible nephew and by default that made me a terrible person. I left them to each other and used the banister rail to pull myself up the stairs. I remember undressing, falling back onto my bed as I took off my jeans, then for some reason deciding to take off my boxers and socks, until I was completely naked. I lay back on my bed on top of the covers and I remember hoping that I'd dream about Eadie not Em, because if I dreamed about Eadie wouldn't that in some way redeem me? Eadie was who I should be dreaming about. A girl close to my age who wasn't my uncle's girlfriend. A girl who I'm sure hadn't hated me on our only meeting. I think I said her name as I closed my eyes but the E of Eadie could have easily slipped into the E of Em as the drink overcame me and I passed out.

I don't know what time it was that I woke but I know what woke me.

Leo, she said.

I wasn't dreaming of Eadie. The voice wasn't hers. It was clipped. It was from a time I didn't know still existed. It was Em's voice.

Her hand was on my chest. I opened my eyes and turned to see that she was in my bed with me. I knew I was naked, but I didn't jump up to cover myself. I was still drunk; the world hadn't stopped spinning.

What are you doing? I heard myself say.

I felt far away from my own body. I could feel her hand moving down my chest to my stomach.

I can't believe you're real, I heard her say.

Her hand caressed my stomach. I could feel myself react.

We can't, I said.

Her other hand touched my cheek.

You feel so beautiful, she said, her body moving closer to me. I felt her lips touch my cheek as she kissed me. I can't believe how perfect you are, she said. You're incredible.

I was drunk and maybe I could blame the drink for what I did next, but the truth was I wanted her, and I wasn't thinking of Toby at all. I was a truly terrible person. I turned to face her and as I did my body pushed her hand lower to my groin and I moved my hand to her body. I felt her skin. My hand touched her breast. She was naked. I kissed her. She kissed me back. Her hand was touching me, and I moved my hand down from her breasts to her stomach. That was my first ever kiss and I'd never even come close to holding a girl's hand yet there I was touching a woman's body.

She stopped kissing me. Her free hand came to my cheek again.

You're impossible, she said. How are you possible?

I just am, I said.

I don't know what I thought she meant. Did I think she had fallen so instantly and insatiably in lust with me? I'm not sure. I just know that I felt that she wanted me, and I wanted her. I wasn't scared, nervous. I always thought I would be. To be honest, I always thought I'd make a mess of my first time, fumble, stumble over what should happen, need her guidance. But in that moment, everything seemed to be happening smoothly, perfectly.

I know this is wrong, she said. I just can't imagine how… I mean, you just are aren't you.

She moved herself on top of me. I think some of the haze of drink must have been wearing off because I was completely aware of her. No dizziness, no swaying. Just the very still moment of looking up at her and seeing her eyes. I remember that. Her eyes. Because I imagined they would be looking at me as I was looking at her, deep into her, but they weren't. She was looking at my arms then my chest, then she lifted my hand and looked from finger to finger, turned my hand over and did the same, then she lifted a lock of my hair up and looked at it, then she began moving on top of me and I was ready to do the same, to copy her, but then something happened that I don't think I would wish on anyone who was about to have sex for the first time.

I knew I wanted to move, to touch her, to make this happen because it seemed it was what we both wanted. No matter that it had come from nowhere. No matter that my uncle was passed out downstairs and Em was his girlfriend. No matter that this was the worst thing I could possibly do. I wanted it.

But it was my body that stopped wanting it. I don't mean I couldn't do it. As Em moved forward to kiss me, I felt that feeling of being far away increase. It was almost like I could feel myself pulling away from myself. The internal from the physical. I wasn't dying, it was more that I could feel my whole body freeze up as if ice was being pumped into my veins and under my skin and into my bones, until I was completely frozen. I don't think Em noticed at first because she kept kissing me. I couldn't feel the kisses, but I knew she was kissing me. I could see her kissing me. I wanted to kiss her. But no matter how much I wanted that I couldn't do anything back. I was locked in myself. I was trapped within a frozen body. Statue-still. Completely unable to move in any way.

Eventually, Em must have realised I wasn't reacting. She sat up and frowned down at me.

Leo, she said. Are you okay? Have I done something wrong?

I couldn't answer. It must have looked crazy to her. I was naked underneath her, my eyes wide open just staring up at her.

She put her hand against my breast. I knew she was feeling for my heartbeat. I knew it was there though I couldn't feel it.

Leo, you're scaring me, she said.

But she didn't jump up. She didn't scream for Toby. She stayed there on top of me looking down into my eyes.

I saw her hand come to my face. I saw her arm moving as she stroked my cheek.

Oh, Leo, she said. I'm so sorry. I shouldn't have done this. I'm sorry. You're so beautiful and impossible, I'm awful for doing this. I'm horrible. Please forgive me, Leo.

I could see she was crying then. That's a nightmare isn't it? The first time I was ever with a woman I made her cry. No one wants that. But even though she was crying, I saw her move her head to mine and I knew she kissed me. I think it was just a light, soft kiss. Then she was climbing off my body. I watched. I saw her standing there naked and then she was beyond my peripheral vision. I heard the door open. I heard the door shut. I couldn't shut my eyes, but I think I must have fallen asleep because in the morning I was woken by a car engine starting and the sudden release from my frozen state made me sit up and take in a desperate breath as if I'd been drowning and managed to free myself from the water. I sat there on my bed, breathing, listening to the car drive off. Don't ask me how but I knew it was Em's car and that I would never see her again.

# Thirteen

Toby was quiet as we drove to Delamere Forest. The snow had fallen heavy all morning and fat white clouds seemed to be lowering over the world. Everything felt heavy and covered. I always find it strange to think that when it snows there's still all that grass underneath the white, that it's alive under there. As we drove north towards the forest, I was looking out at the thick snowfall, and I kept thinking that when it melted this time all the green would be gone. That in its place there would be concrete covering everything, as if while the snow had obscured the ground a change had occurred, one that no one could reverse. Like ripples around the world, I imagined the concrete spreading out and covering everything until there was no grass or flowers or trees. Everything would be trapped beneath that grey layer, unable to free itself, unable to move or breathe.

What'd you think about Em? You liked her, yeah? said Toby as he parked in the forest car park.

I was watching a dad lifting his toddler out of a pram. The toddler was wearing a blue snowsuit. As the dad lifted the little boy, he kind of threw the boy up in the air a little and the toddler laughed as the dad caught him. Even with the window up I could hear that laugh. There was no risk in that moment of flight. The dad was always going to catch him, but as the toddler was thrown up again I wondered what that moment of possibility must feel like, to suddenly feel abandoned, at risk, and yet know you were only an inch away from safety.

She was interesting, I said. I liked her better than your last girlfriend anyway.

Toby was tapping the steering wheel. Oh, come on, you can't bring Camilla up. She was a right bore. I don't know how I stuck with her for so long.

Will you stick with Em? I asked.

I think I wanted the answer to be no. That she was gone. That I would never see her again. That's selfish isn't it? I should have wanted my uncle to be as happy as he could be, not put my own shame or guilt before his contentment.

I don't think she'll stick with me to be honest, Roslin, he said. Just you listen to my wise judgement. The thing about

135

women is you have to at least try to convince them you can stay the way you were when you first met. I'm not saying don't change, I mean that the person you tried your hardest to be in the first few weeks needs to be there somewhere when you get down the line. Got it, Roslin? The problem with your old Uncle Leo is I don't think I have the stamina for that kind of project. It's exhausting trying to keep her hooked on the best of days. I'm a sham, really, I am. I live in this world with these beautiful people, but the sad truth is every moment I spend with them is an effort. It's like I'm Sisyphus. Do you know him? It doesn't matter if you don't, the point is he was this poor bastard who had to carry a rock up a hill and every time he got to the top he had to start over again. I feel like poor bloody Sisyphus whenever I go to a party or reading, I feel like him every time I'm with those people. It's as if I'm carrying that rock up a hill again and again, and I know for a fact that at the next party or lecture or prize-giving it'll start over. So no, Roslin, I don't think I will stick it.

I watched as the dad carried the toddler towards the café. I remembered coming to Delamere with Dad before there was even a café, but he'd bring a flask of tea and some Snowballs. Snowballs were my favourite thing when I was a kid. I used to try to bite the chocolate off the outside so there was only marshmallow. It was impossible and messy, but I never gave up trying.

I think you're giving up too easily, I said. I mean, all those things you just said, the parties and all that, that's why you're down in London isn't it? You love it, so why are you fighting against that? I say just stop trying to carry rocks up a hill.

Toby laughed. You never fail to astound me, Roslin, he said. You know, even when you were little you had an old head on your shoulders.

That's what Mum says, I said.

Oh, is it? She's right then. Sometimes you come out with nuggets of maturity that are way beyond your youthful appearance.

I shook my head. I don't think she means it like that, I said.

How does she mean it then?

I shrugged. I'm not sure, but she never says it when I've said something intelligent or whatever, it's usually just when we're cooking or walking. She'll look at me and tell me that she wishes I wasn't growing up so quickly or that we had more time. It's always pretty emotional, I tend to change the subject.

Ah, I see, said Toby. He tapped the steering wheel again, slower. Well, Mums can get emotional. That's their prerogative after all. But we're men, yeah, so let's put emotion aside and feel the raw reality of nature. What do you say? Shall we venture into the dark forest?

I looked out at the trees. There was nothing dark or mysterious about Delamere. It was all managed paths and marked-out routes.

I might need a coffee first, I said.

It was quiet in the forest. Usually at weekends you can't walk a few yards without passing someone or having a dog that's off its lead sniff at you. As I walked deeper into the forest with Toby, we hardly passed a soul. For a while we followed the path, taking our time, the day too cold to rush. Every time I breathed, I saw my breath expand away from me in a little cloud. Snow fell through the canopy but slower now, just drifts, gentle and meandering in their descent. Eventually Toby whistled and cocked his head to the left away from the path. He clambered over a fallen tree, and I followed him. The ground off the path was soft with layers of snow. My feet fell into it up to my shins. We walked deeper into the trees and as we did, they became denser and there was, in a way, something of the dark forest that Toby had promised about the woods in that space.

Toby was ahead of me, but his pace was slowing. He stopped, knelt in the snow.

What is it? I asked.

He stood up and turned. In each hand he was holding a leaf.

They're a match, he said.

I looked up. I'm not sure what tree it was, the leaves that were left were mostly dead and I couldn't make out their shape with the snow covering them. Besides, I'm not sure I could tell one tree from another. Oak, beech, cedar, pine, the tree could have been any of them.

Aren't all leaves a match? I said.

He was holding the leaves out, so they were on his palm. Both were still a little green with a rusting of red at the outer edges. Both had four parts, four tips.

But look at them, he said, pushing his hands forward. They're completely alike.

I looked. The reddening was covering both leaves at exactly the same point. In the middle of each leaf there was a fleck of black blemish. Even the stems seemed to have been severed from the tree at the same angles. I'm sure if I'd looked closer, I would see more obvious differences but from a brief inspection they did both seem as similar as two different leaves could be.

What do you think? said Toby. Are they the same leaf? Have we walked into a point in our world where parallel universes combine, and these leaves are the evidence of that junction? Or are they twin leaves, fallen at the exact same moment and lying the same way up so that a random passer-by would notice them and see that they were alike? Or are they just different leaves? Do they only seem similar because I want them to seem that way?

This was Toby as his poetic worst. I'd forgotten what he could get like on a walk. I remember last summer, climbing Old Pale with him and looking out towards Manchester. He started talking about the horizon and what it was to feel so exposed to the immeasurable power of the world. In the end, he stopped talking and just looked out into the east as if that immeasurable power had drained all his eloquence. I got what he was saying. I felt it too, standing on that hill and seeing the world, knowing that I was looking towards Manchester but realising I was just a dot on the surface of the planet. I got it, I felt it, I just didn't want to express it like he seemed to need to.

I think they're just different leaves, I said.

I touched the one in his left hand. It was hard, frozen, but I knew if I pressed on it, then it would crumble in its brittleness.

How do we know the answer? he said.

A dog barked somewhere in the trees. I felt snow falling on my hair.

We don't need to know, I said. They're just leaves.

Do we need to know? he said. He closed his fingers on each hand over the leaves, gently. If I just drop them now, couldn't we believe that they were copies of each other? Exactly the same in every way? And if they were would we need to know how that came to be?

He was smiling as he talked. I think sometimes he saw himself as more of a philosopher than a poet.

I think they're just leaves, Toby, I said. The snow was falling heavier. I'd drunk my coffee a mile back along the path and wanted another to warm me.

Look, he said. He opened his fingers and knelt slowly to the snow. Carefully, he turned both leaves over to reveal their reverse. See, he said.

The leaf that had been in his left hand was the same on its reverse. A dying green, blemished with red. But the leaf that had been in his right hand was different. There was no green or red. All of it was black as if that black dot had seeped through and taken over.

Are they still the same leaf? he asked.

I looked at the black leaf. It was dead. There was no

141

doubt about that. I looked at the green leaf and though there was no black on it, it was clear that leaf was just as dead no matter that it was still clinging to an echo of its old greenness.

They're the same, I said. It was instinctive. I'm not saying I believed that the two leaves were copies, it was more I had this sudden understanding that it didn't matter if one was black on one side, that one difference didn't make them different. It was just that something had happened to that leaf which the first had not experienced. That's like identical twins, isn't it? They're born the same but life colours them differently. Changes them, alters the fabric of who they are, so that eventually you could look at those twins when they're eighty and just because you saw how life had physically marked them in different ways, didn't mean that they were never the same to begin with.

Which is more beautiful? said Toby.

Beauty. I think that was Toby's favourite thing in life. He had beautiful girlfriends, he mixed with beautiful people, he lived in a beautiful apartment, he drove a beautiful car, he wrote beautiful poetry, he stood on hills and saw the beauty in the world, he looked at a dead leaf and asked questions about beauty.

That depends, I said.

On what?

On whether they're the same leaf, I said.

I was thinking of the Patterdale, not the one in the field, the one in Australia. The one who wasn't really Buddy, the clone Buddy.

But you think they're the same? he said. Exact copies?

That's just it, I said. If they're copies of each other doesn't that mean that one of the leaves existed first?

I suppose it could.

He was looking up at me, this deep look in his eyes that made me think he was waiting for me to get something, to understand something. All I could think about was Buddy, not the leaves.

If one existed first, I said, that's the only one that contains beauty, isn't it? I mean, the leaf or whatever didn't exist before it existed, but the copy existed after the first. The first one is the true one. That's the one that we should look at and say is beautiful. The other's just a lie, isn't it?

Toby picked up the black leaf. But what if this one *is* the first leaf? What if it didn't exist anymore?

Quickly, he scrunched the leaf in his hand. I could hear it crinkle, crack, break. He opened his hand and little scraps of black fell to the snow.

It's gone, he said. He picked up the other leaf. What does that mean for this leaf?

I thought of Buddy in his Canberra home. I thought of Buddy not knowing he wasn't Buddy. I thought of his owner only having that new Buddy.

I don't know, I said. That's the only one left so if you want to say a dead leaf is beautiful then that's the beautiful one. I just don't think it's more or less beautiful, it's just a leaf.

Toby nodded.

I'm going to keep this one, he said, placing the remaining leaf delicately into his coat pocket.

Come on, he said, standing, his knees wet with snow. I need a coffee now.


Toby let me drive the Jensen home. The roads were clear and even though I don't have a licence, he seemed relaxed sitting next to me in the passenger seat. Every now and again he would say something like ease off a little or careful on this bend, but for the most part he sat not saying a word as the radio played.

It was dark when we got home and as I drove down into the village I had to go slow because the roads hadn't been gritted. As I crawled the Jensen past the church I glanced into the graveyard and saw two figures walking there. One was a man, tall and shaven headed. I could only see him from the side, but I saw he had a tidy black beard. Behind him there was a girl. I know this is going to sound crazy, but as I watched them they stepped forward and vanished. In one moment they were there and in the next they were gone.

Watch it, said Toby and his hand shot to the wheel, steered the Jensen away from the parked Volkswagen I was about to hit.

Sorry, I said. I thought I saw…

Saw what?

Nothing, just a hawk, I think.

Jesus, Roslin. You can't crash just because a hawk flies past. Come on, park up. I'll get some tea on.

I pulled the Jensen up outside my house.

When we were out of the car, I looked back up to the church. Surely people didn't just vanish and if they did, didn't that mean they weren't really there? I don't believe in ghosts. I don't believe in visions or mirages, so even as Toby was opening the front door, I knew I had to know for sure if I'd really seen them vanish. What I wanted was to walk back up to the church and see them both there. They hadn't vanished. They'd just knelt by a grave, laid some flowers, that was all.

I might just go for a bit of a walk, I said.

Toby looked back at me. Shook you up did it? You were way off crashing, I was probably just over-reacting. Okay, I'll get tea sorted while you walk it off.

Thanks, I said. And thanks for letting me drive.

No problem, Roslin, he said as he pushed the door open.

I walked back up the hill. There were lights on in the pub and as I passed, I thought of Em's leg against my leg. It had only been the day before that she'd come, and just like a magic trick you never asked the magician to pull, she was gone. What was she thinking about me now? Did she think I was crazy, damaged in some way? I hoped she'd just forget I existed. Then I could push the embarrassment of that night away, hide it somewhere in my mind where all my other lost memories must be.

As I came into the graveyard, I walked a little slower. I wasn't scared. I didn't believe that I was going to walk right into a phantom, but there was an eerie quiet about the graveyard that wasn't helped by the thick layers of snow covering everything. But that quiet was quickly chased away by the sound of crying. I know how creepy that seems. Sobbing in an empty graveyard late at night. But I kept walking towards the sobbing and when I followed the path around, I saw the girl sat against a gravestone.

At first, I thought the girl was Eadie. She had the same red hair. But as I stepped closer, trying to be as quiet as possible so as not to startle her, I saw that the similarity was only in the hair. I knew who this girl was.

Becca, I said, but the girl didn't look at me. She seemed to not even have heard me. She was sat with her legs outstretched, playing with something in her hand. I stepped closer, not trying to be quiet, half-hoping she'd suddenly startle at my presence. But she didn't react. I was standing right next to her and still she made no move to look at me.

Becca, I said, because I was sure this was Eadie's sister.

She was crying, her body convulsing every now and then as the sobs took control. I knelt beside her. We were so close I could have shaken her shoulder a little, tried to wake her from her reverie. I knew that would do no good. I knew that this was the same girl I'd seen with the man. The man who had vanished. The girl who had vanished. I don't believe in ghosts, but I knew that this was Becca and that she wasn't really there.

She was still playing with whatever was in her hand. I moved closer and was brave enough to lean forward so I could see clearly what she held. She passed it from finger to finger. It was a ring. As she moved it, I saw its head was a silver bee, wings outstretched. She kept moving the ring, crying, wiping her nose. She swallowed as if she could swallow away whatever was upsetting her and stood up. I stood back instinctively. She made no acknowledgement of my presence. She turned to face the grave and like that she let the ring drop. The grave was covered in snow, but I saw the ring clearly pass through that snow to rest on the stone beneath. Becca was still crying, her body shaking. I saw her mouth move and knew she was speaking but I couldn't hear the words. Then something must have startled her because she turned away from me. I looked to see where she was looking. Next to the gates was the man with the beard. He was nothing but shadow, faint, like fog. I strained my eyes to try to see him but as I did, he faded until there was no man, only the gate and the night and the snow falling. I turned to Becca, but she was gone too.

I looked down at the grave. The ring had fallen not into the snow but through it, and though I knew it was a crazy thing to do, I fell to my knees and started clearing the freezing snow from the base of the gravestone. I felt the ring before I saw it.

When I pulled the ring out of the snow, part of me hoped that it wouldn't be the same ring. If it wasn't the same, I could tell myself I'd imagined everything and question later why that was happening to me, why my mind seemed to be playing tricks on me all the time. If the ring was real then that would mean I had to accept that I'd seen Becca, that I'd seen the bearded man. That even though they weren't really there they were real. I looked at the ring.

The band was silver. The head was a silver bee with wings outstretched.

# *Fourteen*

I don't want what I did next to be misconstrued.

First off, it wasn't my intention to go anywhere near Eadie's house. What I was intending to do was take the book Toby had given me and walk into Northwich, find somewhere to sit, and at least try to read it. What Toby had said about not trying to find answers all the time was playing on my mind. All night I hadn't been able to sleep. I was thinking of the runner and the hawk, the ghosts who I knew couldn't be ghosts, my crazy dreams. I couldn't stop trying to find answers, so when it was morning the first thing I did was to find the book and tell myself that I needed to block out any search for answers. More than that, I think I wanted to block out that there even was a runner or a hawk or impossible ghosts. I still had the ring in my jeans pocket, so when I walked out of my house with

*The Anathemata* shoved into my coat, I think it was the ring that made me turn left not right, so that instead of walking down High Street, I walked up towards the church and Eadie's house. All the time my hand was in my pocket, moving the bee ring around just as Becca had, and before I knew it, I was standing at Eadie's front door about to ring the bell.

It wasn't that I was using the opportunity of finding the ring to get close to Eadie. That wasn't it at all. In fact, if I'm honest, after what happened with Em I really don't think I wanted to be so close to a woman again for a long time just to avoid messing up, so it wasn't as if I was going to give her the ring and expect a date or something in return. When you think about it, that would be pretty sick. If something had really happened to Becca, then I would have been using that to get close to Eadie. I'm not like that. I thought she should have the ring, or at least as I stood on her doorstep pressing the doorbell, that's what I told myself.

It was early, but it hadn't crossed my mind that anyone but Eadie would open the door. As I stood waiting, I started to panic that her dad might be the one who opened the door to me. I'd never seen her dad, but I had this image of him being very severe looking, stern, and judgemental, asking me what my intentions were with his daughter. I was about to turn and walk away when the door opened.

Oh, hello weirdo, said Eadie.

She was still in her pyjamas, her hair tied up, her feet bare on the hall tiles. I felt like I shouldn't be seeing her in her pyjamas, but she was bouncing a little on her toes almost like she was excited to see me.

Did you spy on me until you saw my dad leave? she said, head tilting with a grin.

What? No, I said. I just found something I thought you might want.

Interesting, she said. So, let's get this right, you thought you'd bring it over and I'd invite you in and we'd do stuff. Is that it?

She was still grinning, so I knew she was joking, but I was sure I was blushing. Don't get me wrong, the image of her inviting me in and doing stuff was embarrassing but I was more nervous because now I was there, I suddenly realised I had no choice but to give her the ring and then what if she asked questions about how I found it? Would I have to tell her about what I saw? Would she believe me if I just said I'd found it?

Don't be silly, I said. I pulled the ring out and held it to her. I found this that's all and I was thinking about what you said about your sister and bees.

Her face was as white as the snow that was everywhere. She stopped bouncing.

Shit, she said, grabbing the ring from my hand. Where? Seriously, what the hell? You found this? Where, Leo, where?

As she spoke, I saw there were tears in her eyes. I thought of Becca sobbing alone in the graveyard. Why was she crying? Was it the bearded man? Was he making her cry? Those questions raced through my mind as Eadie brought the ring to her lips and kissed it.

It was in the graveyard, I said, pointing randomly towards the graves. I was walking through, and I saw it there on the path.

I know that was a lie but what else could I say? I couldn't say I saw a ghost cast it away into the snow, that I dug through that snow until I felt the sharp little wings scrape my finger.

She looked over to the graveyard.

There? All this time? I don't understand. This was her favourite. She'd never take it off, not on purpose. Do you know what this means?

I wanted to tell her that she would take it off on purpose,

153

that she had, that I'd seen her do just that, but how could I say that?

What does it mean? I said, dreading the answer.

She kissed the ring again. It means whoever hurt her must have dropped this and that means everything must have happened here. Oh God, that's so horrible, I feel sick. Will you come in? I feel like I might be sick.

She didn't give me a chance to answer. She pulled on my arm until I was inside, shut the door behind us and started running up the stairs.

When she was halfway up, she stopped and looked back. I was still stood in the hallway.

Come on then, she said.

She ran up the rest of the stairs. Even though I swear this was not what I imagined would happen no matter how unbelievable that sounds, I followed her.

Upstairs, there was a large landing with framed abstract art on the wall. For some reason I thought a vicar would have paintings of Jesus everywhere, but Eadie's house was very minimalist. All the walls were a clean white and the paintings, three of them on the wall between Eadie's bedroom and the bathroom, were in white frames. Eadie went into her room, so I followed. It was nothing like the room from my dream. That room had been neat, organised into one theme.

Whereas the rest of the house was all precise lines and white space, this room seemed to be where everything that was unwanted had been dumped. This room was a barrage of chaotic clashes. The bed wasn't four-poster, it was a divan, and the sheets were a mess of blankets piled with too many cushions on top. There were posters on the walls, but not the posters I would have expected for someone Eadie's age. There was one of David Bowie, another of Kate Bush, then here and there, blue-tacked without any sense of order, were posters of eighties films. There was *The Breakfast Club*, *Say Anything*, *Heathers*, *Sixteen Candles* and *The Dark Crystal*. There was an armchair in the far corner that was covered in T-shirts, jumpers, and skirts, and beneath that mess I could see a tangle of teddies buried. There was a dressing table, but the mirror was covered with stickers and Post-it notes, what glass that wasn't covered was obscured with a layer of dust and grime. The table itself was strewn with empty Lucozade and Coke bottles, a vape, sweet packets, dirty bean-smeared plates, and schoolbooks. There was a Yankee candle burning, giving the room a soft vanilla scent. I stood just inside the doorway as Eadie threw herself flat on her bed, still holding the ring in both hands, staring at it like she couldn't believe it existed. Maybe she felt like the ring was some part of Becca returned to her. I had this awful feeling then. Had I made the grief she must have been dealing with for years, that kind of mirage grief where there's nothing precise to grieve over, not actual death just an absence of somebody who was there and was no longer there, a grief for the missing, suddenly return to her afresh, shining like the silver bee so she couldn't look away from it?

I can't believe you found this, she said, turning onto her back. Sit down, you can't just stand in my doorway like a freak. We need to shut the door anyway in case Dad comes back.

Do we? I said.

She nodded. Yeah, of course we do. What do you think he'd do if he found a random boy in my room? You do realise you're going out the window if he comes back? He's only in church, he could be back at any moment really. I don't quite know why I invited you in. You can climb, can't you?

I looked across the room to the sash window. I don't think so, I said.

Oh well, just shut the door and come sit down. She patted the bed and sat herself up against the mountain of cushions.

I shut the door as she asked, made my way across the room, trying not to stand on a plate of half-eaten cottage pie. When I got to the bed I perched on the edge, as far away from her as I could, but straight away she jumped up and sat herself right next to me, our shoulders touching.

Tell me then, she said. Were you a being a detective for me or did you really just find it? Proper kismet.

I thought of the ghosts in the night. The man with the beard. Becca crying. The ring falling through the snow as if there were no snow.

Honestly, I said. I just found it lying there.

Do you always walk through graveyards? You're not a goth, are you?

She pushed her body against mine. She was still holding the ring on her lap, one finger caressing the bee as she spoke to me.

Only when I need to dig up a body, I said.

She laughed. You're a proper weirdo aren't you, Weirdo? Don't worry, I'm always walking there. There's nowhere else to walk in this stupid village where you can just be alone is there? And if anyone sees me, I just pretend I'm there to visit my dead mum or something. I stop at a grave and look at it all sad and solemn. I even cry sometimes. I can do that on demand if I want. Can you?

She spoke so fast, her legs jittering as she spoke.

Not on demand, I said. I think I'd need to at least feel something.

Like your sister dying or something? she said.

I don't have a sister.

How sad. Are you a poor only child? You kind of look like an only child now I think about it. I suppose we both are now; my sister is probably, definitely, dead and you've always been alone. We're both lonely only kids. How utterly sad.

I quite like being an only child. There's no one to bother you.

Or get better Christmas presents. God, Becca always got the better presents. She was definitely Dad's favourite, at least until she started rebelling, she was. She definitely wasn't his favourite when she was staying out all night, going off with boys from Rudheath. Oh well, I suppose I'm the favourite now.

Not if he catches me here, I said.

She laughed and elbowed my arm.

Why? Are we going to have sex? Is that why you found the ring, so you could seduce me?

She did something crazy then. She jumped up and stood in front of me then she came forward and with one hand pushed me back, and before I could do anything she was straddling me.

What if he came in now? she said. What would you do?

I lay there, her body on top of me as she looked down. A few strands of her red hair had fallen over her face. Her cheeks were flushed, I'm sure mine were too. It had come from nowhere, but I felt like she was waiting for me to start something.

He's not here though, I said.

She raised an eyebrow. No, he's not. And I'm all alone with a grave-walking weirdo.

I don't know where the courage came from, but I put my hands on her hips, just placed them there. She did another eyebrow raise.

Are you going to try to kiss me? she said.

I don't even know you, I said and as I spoke her hands came to lay on top of mine. She felt warm.

You're a mystery, she said and then without giving me a chance to be braver, she lowered her body towards me and kissed me. It wasn't just one quick kiss. She pushed her lips against mine and I kissed her back. Em doesn't count. I was too drunk when she kissed me, so I think this was my first real kiss. She tasted of toothpaste and even though I didn't have a clue what to do, I was kissing her back, our mouths opening, tongues touching. My hands were still on her hips but one of hers was in my hair while the other was on my stomach. We kept kissing. Time didn't matter. I didn't care

159

if her dad was about to burst in. I don't think I would have noticed. Eventually, I moved my hands, one to her hair, copying her, and the other to her bum. I don't know how you breathe when you kiss for that long, but our lips didn't part and the more we kissed the more our hands moved over each other's bodies, until hers was undoing my jeans, pushing itself down to touch me so I copied, moved my hand underneath her pyjamas until I could feel her underwear.

Suddenly, she broke our kiss and pulled away. She was breathing hard. My hand was still on her bum. Hers had left my body.

Enough, she said, biting her lip. Do you agree?

She jumped off me, fixed her pyjamas, went to the dusty mirror, wiped away the dirt and fixed her hair. I just lay there. I wasn't frozen like I was with Em, thankfully that hadn't happened, and the thing was I didn't even think about it happening while Eadie was kissing me. This was a different kind of frozen. I was in shock, I think. I just had to lie there and conceptualise what had happened, what I had felt as she kissed me.

That was fun, she said, grabbing her phone from a side table and throwing herself back against her cushions. You can come sit next to me if you want. No kissing though.

I nodded. Yeah, just give me a minute.

She laughed. Oh God, are you that turned on? Have I broken you?

I sat up. Sometimes, in the middle of the night I wake up and even though it's silent, no noise at all, I can hear my heart beating in my ears. Its's too loud, too fast, and when I get out of bed to get some water, my movements all feel too fast but also far away from myself. I've never told anyone about it, not even Mum and Dad. It's been getting worse in the last year, happens every week or so. What I have to do is just sit on my bed and close my eyes, try to slow my breathing even though I don't think my breathing is in reality fast. The more I listen to the sound of my heart in my ears the more I realise it isn't my heart beating. It's something else. It gets faster and faster, louder and louder, and then just like that it stops.

As I sat up on Eadie's bed, I was panicking that same thing was about to happen. I could feel my heart racing. I closed my eyes. There was no beating in my ears. I put my hand on my chest, breathed, felt my heart slow.

Are you having a heart attack, Weirdo? she said. Please don't, my dad would kill me if you died in here. He'd probably have to do your funeral too, that would be so awkward. Come on, sit up next to me, I want to tell you something.

I'm fine, I said. Just a bit...

Excited, I know. I'm incredible, aren't I. Maybe I'll kiss you again someday.

Maybe I'll kiss you again, I said.

She giggled. Of course you will.

She moved along the bed, and I sat next to her. It was me sitting as close to her as she had been to me earlier now, and she didn't move away.

So, listen, she said. I did some investigating too.

About your sister?

Nope, she said, leaning her head on my shoulder. I like how you smell. Anyway, I did some investigating about you.

You did? Why?

I felt her shrug. Because I thought you were weird, couldn't figure out why I'd never seen you before. I asked my dad first, but he was very sketchy.

You asked him about me? What did he say?

She shrugged again. Not much. He confirmed your story at least. He said he knew your dad was called Perry and your mum was called Sophie, but they never came to church. He said you were probably Catholics or something. Are you? I don't think he likes Catholics, though he'd never admit that.

We're not anything, I said. Did he mention me?

162

She shook her head. Nope. He said he didn't know if the pagan Roslins had a kid, that they could, that your house was nice. Did you know a famous BBC radio DJ used to live there in the eighties?

I didn't know that, I said. Is that all you found out?

The scent of vanilla in the air had been lessened by how familiar I'd grown with her scent. It was remnant perfume, unwashed hair that didn't smell unclean, the memory too of the taste of her kiss. I almost felt like we'd known each other for ages, our bodies so close together and naturally relaxed.

I'm a very good detective, she said. I found out lots more. I asked all my friends about you. I asked if anyone knew a weirdo called Leo.

You really said that?

Maybe. Maybe I just said Leo. Anyway, don't interrupt. You interrupt me far too much. The fact is, none of them knew any Leo from school or from round here, but my friend Cassie, she has a sister your age called Madi. Do you know a Madi? Well, Madi says she went to reception with a boy called Leo, but he died when he was like five she said. That's sad, isn't it?

Very, I said. But that couldn't be me.

Nope. That Leo definitely isn't you.

Was that everything?

She sighed. Alas, yes. That was the end of my investigation. You know what that means, don't you?

What does it mean?

That you're not only a weirdo, you're a proper mystery too. I like mysteries.

She looked up at me. I think we were about to kiss. It was a very charged, intense moment. Our eyes looking into each other's, willing the other to kiss, but then there was a sound downstairs, a door opening.

Oh shit, she said, jumping up. Dad's back. Ready to climb, Leo?

You're not serious?

No other way out, she said. She ran to her bedroom door and locked it.

Quick, she said. Window, now.

I've never climbed out of a window in my life. Never climbed into a window. In fact, I don't think I've even climbed a tree. I thought of how cold it was outside, all the ice out there. But what choice did I have?

Eadie ran across the room. Her dad shouted something.

I'm just getting dressed, she called in a sweet voice. Hurry up, Leo. She lifted the window, cold air shooting in and making the candle flicker.

I joined her at the window, peered out. We were only

one storey up, but the drop to the garden might as well have been from the top of a block of flats.

There's a trellis, she said. All you have to do is climb down it. Dad'll be in the kitchen, so he won't see you, hopefully. You're not heavy, are you? It's not like you'll break the trellis.

I was only half-listening to her, peering down into what seemed an abyss.

Ready? she said.

Probably not, I said, but I was already climbing out of the window, one leg forward, my hand groping around for the criss-cross wood of the trellis.

You're so brave, she said, a whispered laugh.

I'm really not, I said.

She leaned forward and kissed me on my cheek. You are kind of. Now, quick. He'll see you if you don't hurry up.

I had no choice. My fingers found the trellis and I managed to pull the rest of my body out of the window without freezing with fear. Everything was cold. The wood was cold, the morning air seemed to immediately attack my fingers, threatening my precarious grip. I looked down, told myself it wasn't far.

This reminds me of *Romeo and Juliet*, said Eadie as I started to lower myself down.

Is it that romantic? I said, not daring to look up at her.

Not romantic, she said. I meant the bit where Romeo climbs out of Juliet's window. That's not romantic, it's the last time she sees him really. She imagines he's in a tomb.

I lowered myself again, looked down. The best option was to drop and let the snow cushion my fall.

Are you saying I'm going to die? I said.

But she didn't answer. Her window shut quickly, and I heard banging on her door. I took one last look down and tried to pretend I wasn't afraid, then let go.

I didn't fall like a brick. I managed to push myself back. There was plenty of grass beneath me, all of it covered in snow. In that split second, I closed my eyes and waited for the ground to smack into me.

It didn't smack into me. I landed with a dull thud. The snow was soft, and the fall hadn't been long enough. I was fine. I lay there on the snow like I'd lain on her bed, looking up at the crystal-clear winter sky. It had stopped snowing.

When I stood, I looked up to Eadie's window. Part of me wanted to see her there, checking if I was safe, blowing me a kiss. But there was no one at the window. I started walking up the path, out of her garden, and it was only when I got to the church that I realised someone was behind me.

Hold on there, shouted a voice.

166

I glanced back. There was a tall man in a long waterproof coat striding towards me. He was stern looking, gaunt almost.

I kept walking and he called again.

I said hold on, he shouted. I heard him running then, and before I could run, his hand was on my shoulder, spinning me round.

Beneath the coat I could see the white of a dog collar.

I don't think a man of God should have looked at me with the hate I saw in his eyes. His teeth were gritted like a dog. He grabbed me by the collar of my coat.

I know you, he said, spit spraying my face.

I tried to pull free but for a skinny man he was strong.

I didn't do anything, I said. I could hear how pathetic my own voice sounded.

You listen, he said, pulling me closer to his face. You stay away from my daughter. You got that? Stay the hell away. That's the only warning you'll get.

He gripped my collar harder, tightening it about my throat.

I brought my hand up to try to pull his away, but at that moment someone else was shouting.

Get off him! a voice called.

I couldn't turn to see who it was but with a second shout,

Eadie's dad let go of me and I fell to the snow-covered cobbles.

I was vaguely aware of someone else standing over me. I heard voices shouting. I saw shapes moving, someone push someone else. Someone called my name. I knew it was Toby, but I couldn't answer.

I wasn't frozen. It was the opposite. I was on the floor and every part of me was moving uncontrollably, spasming, fitting. Everything was black and I could taste blood on my lips. I wanted the spasming to stop but it wouldn't. I felt like I was being shook faster and faster. I don't know if I cried or shouted out. I felt a hand on my chest. I felt my body being turned on its side. I felt someone push their fingers into my mouth. I heard a mumbled voice. *Keep away from him.* I heard Toby's voice. It's okay, Leo. It'll be okay. Stay calm. Listen to my voice. You're okay. But I kept spasming and I was convinced my body was going to pull itself apart, that my sinews would burst, my muscles split, and I was going to die. I gave in to that thought. Everything was black. Everything made sense. The dreams. The runner. The hawks. The ghosts. I was broken. There had been something terribly wrong with me and now this was the end point. I was dead.

# Fifteen

Toby must have carried me inside because when I woke it was dark. The television was on with the sound off. I could see the new Doctor Who being interviewed on the *One Show*. The presenters and the new Doctor were laughing. For some reason there was a dachshund on the coach next to the presenter and the dachshund was biting its tail. I sat up, my body feeling like I'd been through twelve rounds with a heavyweight boxer. A sharp stab of pain shot through my head. I put my hands to my temple, the stab came again. I think I must have groaned because Toby came running in. He had on Dad's apron with the cats all over it, a joke birthday present from Mum. When did she give him that? I narrowed my eyes, saw the cats playing with yarn on the apron, tried to remember how long ago it was that Mum had given the apron to Dad, tried to remember that moment

169

of him unwrapping the present, seeing the cats, seeing that it was an apron, the incredulity then the uncontrollable laughter. But there was a gap where that memory should have been, only the knowledge that it was a gift remained.

Woah there, Roslin, said Toby, sitting himself in the armchair beside me.

I rubbed my fingers at my temples. The pain had gone but I knew the agony had started there. I wanted to stop it happening again, so I pressed harder, scrunching up my eyes. I remembered Eadie's dad grabbing me, the quick understanding that I wasn't in control of my body, the shaking, the fit.

What's happening to me, Toby? I said.

I started crying then. I know how pathetic that is, but I couldn't stop myself. Floods of tears fell. I was shaking as I cried, not like before, just shaking and shaking. Toby moved from the couch to the floor beside the sofa. He took my hands away from my temples, squeezed them into his.

Hey, hey, come on, he said. This is silly. You're fine. You've just had a little fit that's all. It's okay, Roslin. I'm here.

I had a flash of memory. Toby talking to Mum, promising her he'd be there for me. Why would he need to be there for me?

I was shaking my head. No, it's not okay. Why did Mum and Dad leave me? There's something wrong with me isn't there? There was that kid, what did I do, Toby? I don't understand, I don't get what's going on.

Toby squeezed my hands again, kissed them.

Don't say that. You're fine, there's nothing wrong with you. They didn't leave you; they'd never do that. It was me, I told them to go. Do you hear me, Roslin? It was me, I told them to leave you because I knew how difficult it was.

I shook my head again, harder, as if shaking my head would bring clarity.

What? Why would you do that? Why would you tell them to go away if there wasn't something wrong with me? It's not just the kid and the fit, Toby. I'm seeing stuff, weird stuff, and none of it makes sense. Why would everything be frozen? I don't get it, I don't get it.

Toby pulled me towards him, held me tight.

You listen to me, he said. None of this is your fault. Wait there, I need to give you something and then we can talk. Okay? Just stop blaming yourself, it's not you, Leo. Listen to me, this isn't your fault.

He let go of me and I collapsed into the couch. I closed my eyes. I felt suddenly detuned, out of phase and separate from myself. I closed my eyes harder. Shook my head. He was wrong. It wasn't okay, nothing was. I hadn't told him about the ghosts because why would anyone admit to that? That's madness, isn't it? To say I've been seeing ghosts, that one of them dropped a ring and I found the ring exactly where she dropped it. I was mad, that must have been what was happening. My brain was breaking down. I was losing it. In the darkness of my closed eyes, I saw the shadowy shape of a hawk, wings unmoving, and then I saw a man stuck in the act of running. I opened my eyes, and they were gone.

Toby came back in. I saw him through tear-soaked eyes. He was holding a soft toy rabbit in his hand.

He handed the rabbit to me. It was midnight blue, and its eyes were a lighter, paler blue.

Do you remember him? he asked.

No, I said. The rabbit was old. One of its ears had been sewn back on and now I held him I saw one of his paws was missing.

Are you sure? said Toby. What if I told you his name?

I looked at the rabbit. Its pale-blue eyes looked like they were full of glitter, they sparkled like they held little galaxies inside.

Rabalon, said Toby. You remember now, don't you?

I shook my head.

I really thought you might, he said. Or at least I hoped seeing Rabalon would, I don't know, help me tell you.

Tell me what?

There was silence. I could hear that Toby was crying. Not like me, not uncontrollable sobs, just a cry that he was trying to hold in. I heard him take a deep breath as if he were readying himself for something.

Tell me, Toby, I said. Please. I know something's wrong; I just need to know what that something is.

Toby took another breath, looked up at me. His eyes were red. I'd never seen my uncle cry, there'd never been a time where I could envisage him needing to.

He spoke slowly, his voice only slightly quivering. I want you to know we all love you, he said.

I know that, I don't need you saying that shit to me. Just tell me what's wrong with me.

Just listen, even when I've told you this, I want you to know nothing has ever changed in how we feel about you. You are and always have been our Leo. Everything I'm about to tell you, I want you to keep remembering that one truth. You are our Leo. Promise me?

I wasn't crying anymore. I was holding the rabbit close to my chest like a toddler would. It was soft and smelt musty like it had been in a box for years.

I promise, I said.

Okay, I think I have to start with Rabalon then, he said. I wish you remembered him. Christ, you used to love that rabbit, wouldn't go anywhere without him. I remember you came down to London when you were about three, your mum and dad were going out to a work thing of your mum's, and I was designated babysitter. We had a great night. You made me watch *101 Dalmatians* with you about three times, then at bedtime you were knackered, but you started asking for Rabby and I had no idea what you meant. Five minutes later you were screaming for this bloody Rabby. I tried calling your mum and dad, but they didn't answer, so there I was with you screaming for hours for Rabby. You must have cried yourself out in the end, fell asleep on my chest so I didn't dare move until your mum and dad came in at five.

I don't remember, I said.

I know you don't. That's okay. I get it now. It was Rabalon that started all of this.

All of what?

He ignored my question. He wasn't looking at me. As he talked, his head had dropped.

It was a bad winter, worst we'd had for years. Your mum had flu, your dad had been away with work. It was your fifth birthday, of course you were excited. I mean you were hard work on the best of days, always wanted someone to play with, to build LEGO with, so imagine what you were like on your birthday. It was a Tuesday, close to Christmas, so I wasn't teaching. I was down in Hull then, just finished my PhD. Your mum rang me at about six in the morning, said Perry wouldn't be back until five that night, could I come up, she was exhausted. I left right away, drove non-stop, but by the time I got to Great Budworth, your dad was there, managed to get an earlier flight I think. Your mum was a wreck, so me and your dad decided to get you out. It was late afternoon, still a bit of light, so I drove us down to the Blue Bridge. We used to walk down there loads when you were in the pram, and I hadn't been for ages. I suppose that makes it all my fault. I've never thought about that really, but going there was my idea. Jesus. So, we walk down by the river, it's freezing, you've got Rabalon, won't let go of him. Me and your dad are talking about football, he was meant to be driving down to Cardiff to watch City play but the way your mum was he was thinking of cancelling. I'd been to Goodison the week before. I think we got distracted by that, but then again you were a fast little sod. You didn't get far away from us, not really. I don't know how it happened. There were some moorhens and you

175

never liked them much, there was a dog off its lead, so I'm not sure if you got scared, but the next thing I knew you were crying and Rabalon wasn't in your hands, and then you were there one minute on the bank of the river, next you were gone. Right through the ice. Just like that. We were right in after you, I swear we were. I went in first, dived through that bloody ice, didn't even feel how cold it was till after. Have you ever been in a river when it's iced over? It was pitch black in there. I couldn't see a thing; I was just flailing my arms about screaming your name. Then I heard your dad jump in and we were both there screaming for you. You'd think we'd find you straight away. I mean we were in about a minute after you, jumped in right where you fell. Your dad found Rabalon but there was no sign of you. I'm no swimmer but I dived right down. It's not deep and I didn't care if I'd drown, I had to find you. I was grabbing and grabbing and then I felt your leg, I knew it was your leg. I pulled on you, dragged you out. Your dad was there next to me, we hauled you out, near threw you onto the bank. There was a crowd around us by then, the man with his dog, a young couple, and then this young guy running towards us shouting he was a nurse. Me and your dad were shivering, we could hardly move. Coats were thrown over us and we just sat there, watched as the nurse started doing CPR on you. Jesus, Roslin, you were white as a sheet. Your eyes were closed, you looked so tiny. I remember your dad crawling to you and putting Rabalon in your little hand, but you didn't react. The nurse kept doing CPR. The people around us were crying. I could hear someone on their phone to an ambulance. I was still just sitting in the same spot, numb, frozen. I couldn't do anything. I hadn't saved you. I was your uncle, I was meant to protect you, but I hadn't.

I reached for Toby's hand.

It's okay, I said. You saved me. I'm here, I'm alive.

He couldn't hold the tears in anymore. That's just it, Roslin. I couldn't save you, none of us could. You died right there on that riverbank. Your dad was in bits when the nurse stopped doing compressions. It took the ambulance another ten minutes to turn up, all that time your dad just lay beside you holding you. No one could get him off you. You were dead, Roslin. You are dead.

I stared at Rabalon. The rabbit's plastic eyes looked like little frozen pools of ice. I imagined myself in them, drowning over and over. Imagined, not remembered.

I'm dead, I said.

I thought of Eadie's kiss. I'd felt that. It was real. Surely you can only feel something if you're alive? I thought of the ghosts, phantoms that shouldn't have been there. I saw myself as a phantom. Misty, faint, fading.

No, said Toby. I mean yes, in a way, yes. You're dead, Roslin. Or at least *that* you is dead. Five-year-old you on that riverbank died and none of us could save you or bring you back.

But I'm here, I said.

I don't think I was saying the words to Toby. I was saying them to myself, telling myself that I was real, that I was Leo Roslin, that I existed, that I lived.

You're here because of your dad, said Toby.

He was looking right at me now. It was as if telling that story, getting it all off his chest, had released something, some pressure he must have been carrying for nearly thirteen years.

He saved me? I said.

It was hope. I wanted Toby to say, yes, in the end he saved you. When everyone else had given up on you, when the paramedics couldn't do anymore, your dad saved you. That he kept trying and he brought you back. But Toby didn't tell me any of that.

He brought you back to us, said Toby. Your mum was a mess, I don't think she would have coped without you for much longer, but about six months after you died

178

something amazing happened. Your dad was working for Foresight Nickson. You know what they do right? AI, new technologies, cutting-edge stuff.

Patterdales, I said, because I remembered then. The article about the Australian dog, Buddy, had named the company who was creating cloned pets. Dad's company. Foresight Nickson.

What? said Toby. No, not Patterdales. People, Roslin. In those days cloning was relatively new, had only just been ratified by the Oslo Convention. It was all over the papers but like anything else you had to be ridiculously rich to pay for the privilege. Your mum and dad weren't millionaires. Euros Nickson was, and Euros Nickson liked your dad a lot. Everyone likes your dad, but Euros trusted your dad. So, when he saw what a mess your dad had become without you, I think he couldn't help but try to help in the only way he really could. He came to this house himself; I was here. He sat in this very room on the sofa you're lying on now and he told them what he was willing to do. He said he could clone you. He said he could bring you back at exactly the same age you left us. Can you imagine that Roslin? Can you imagine how we all felt? It was like God coming down and saying they'd made a mistake, that they were sending you back. No one gets that chance, no one.

What did they say? I asked. I knew the answer. Of course, they said yes. I knew it because I could feel it in my stomach. I wanted to be sick. I wanted to leave the living room and go somewhere and vomit and forget everything Toby was saying. Deny it. Refuse it. I was Leo Roslin. I wasn't a copy. I was the only Leo Roslin, I knew that I was. But then deep down I also knew I wasn't. I knew something wasn't right in me, that there were too many gaps in my being, in my sense of who I was, in my memories. What Toby was saying gave an answer to those flaws. Why wouldn't you remember your childhood? Because you never lived it. Another you did. You only came along after that life had been lived. You were a copy. An imposter. A replicant of the real you.

They did what any parent would do, said Toby. They said yes.

I laughed. So, I'm the property of Foresight Nickson? Am I like some kind of product they've loaned out?

Don't be silly, you're you. You're their son. You're my nephew. You're Leo.

He held my hand, but I pulled it away immediately.

No, I'm not. You just told me I'm not. You said Leo died. You said you saw me, him, die. You said it yourself, I'm a copy made in a factory.

I was crying again. I hate crying. I hardly ever cry and

180

when I do I feel like a baby who isn't in control of his emotions. But I didn't care. I was angry, my tears weren't sadness or pity, they were tears of anger. How dare they all lie to me for so long. How dare they make the choice to remake me like I'm some pet, like I'm a Patterdale. I was a human being. I'd died. Why couldn't they have just left me dead? Grieved me. Loved the memory of me. Mourned the future I never had. That's what everyone else had to do when they lost someone. But, no, my parents had been given a chance to play God, so they took that chance. I wasn't the son they had wanted.

You're not a copy, said Toby. You're you. Listen to me, you're you and we love you. Your mum and dad brought you back because they couldn't live without you. Do you realise how much love it takes to make that choice?

Love? How is it love to lie to me all these years?

They didn't lie to you, Roslin. What did you want them to do? Tell you straight away? When is a good time to tell someone that? They were protecting you.

I looked up at Toby. I think I was hoping to see him smiling like this was all some kind of sick joke, but he wasn't smiling, he was a mess. His eyes raw. He wanted me to understand as if this was something someone could ever understand.

Do you remember what happened after that stuff with the kid at the lake?

Nothing, I said. We just went home. We never even talked about it.

No, that's not right. They took you home and you had a fit, just like before. You slept for a week. They couldn't even move you. Your body was rigid, so they just had to leave you right there on the living-room floor where you fell. When you woke, you had no memory of the kid or even sleeping. They took you straight to Foresight Nickson. Do you remember?

I had no memory of any of what he was talking about.

They drove you down to Loughborough to NIX, that's one of their big research labs. Euros was there himself, flew over from Geneva. Do you remember him?

I shook my head.

They did tests on you. You were there for two weeks, Roslin.

I shook my head again. What he was saying couldn't have been right. He was telling me something that had happened in my own life and I had absolutely no memory at all of any of it. No lab. No scientists prodding at me. No tests. Nothing.

It's okay, I think that's all part of what's happening to you, he said. Your body's way of coping. You're blocking things out.

Why would I do that?

Toby sat on the sofa, his body almost collapsing into the cushions, exhausted.

Because of what they found.

And what was that?

I hated these questions he was leading me to ask him. I didn't want an answer to any of them. I wanted to do what he'd said I'd already done. To lie down on the carpet and sleep, not for a week this time, not for a month. I wanted to sleep forever.

They told your mum and dad there was a chance you weren't well. The word they used was failing.

As soon as he said that word, I knew what I had to do. This couldn't just be a story I was being told. It was my life, whatever that life actually was, and I knew that I couldn't keep letting others know the truth of that life while I stayed in an ignorant darkness. I was sick of the dark.

Stop, I said.

But he didn't stop. When they made you, they said you had years ahead of you, a whole life. A five-year-old clone with a future the same as any other five-year-old. There was no way your mum and dad could ever have known, ever believed…

I said stop. I don't need to hear anything else. I want to go there.

Go where? said Toby but even as he asked the question a sudden realisation dawned. Oh no, you don't want to do that, mate. It's not right. I mean it's just that wouldn't help you.

Nothing he could have said would have changed my mind.

I'm going to Foresight Nickson, I said. If I'm failing then they can tell me why and if they made me then they can fix me.

But Leo, your mum and dad tried. They went there. It's not as simple as…

I stood up. I swayed a little as I did but as Toby went to grab my arm, I pushed him away.

I'm going there now, I said. Please.

# Sixteen

We drove out through lanes that cut through fields beyond Winsford. The drive reminded me of those trips to the hospital with Dad. Neither of us admitting the importance of the journey. Neither of us speaking for fear our voices might break the spell of delay. Time isn't real if you deny it even exists. The drive didn't take half an hour but as we drove, I didn't say one word to Toby. I looked out of the window at the flat land and fields that seemed to stretch like one great frozen lake of whiteness into the horizon. I imagined myself running across those fields. Not racing, not fleeing, just gently running over that consistent landscape, separate from everything around me, each step taking me further and further away from the truth of my life. But as we turned towards a place called Wettenhall, I saw the runner-me continue in one direction while we followed a different road.

Foresight Nickson was an anomaly suddenly appearing as if from nowhere to dominate the flat Cheshire plain. It sat low in a dip, a mile or so back from the road we were on, but as we drove closer it seemed to rise like a black iceberg pushing itself free of a frozen sea. I sat up a little in the car seat. I think Toby was about to say something as we turned onto the private road that led to the Foresight Nickson complex, but we hit a speedbump and he swore and slowed down.

The main building stood at the end of the long private road. There was a heavily fortified fence across the field that intersected the road. A security building stood at the main gate and beside that, on either side of the road, were two identical steel structures. At first, I thought they were both figure eights pushed on to their sides, the bright winter sun gleaming off the steel. But as we got closer, I saw that the steel held detail. Scales, almost too fine to see, and where the two circles of eight met I saw what looked like the head of a snake, its steel eyes glazed, vacant, eating its own tail.

Toby brought the car to a stop and wound down his window. A tall security guard in a heavy high-vis coat came towards the car. As Toby spoke to him, I looked ahead of us to the main building. It was a pyramid, black glass towering unnaturally into the sky. It reminded me of some kind of futuristic cathedral, so big and at odds with its surroundings that it couldn't have ever been meant to have been anything but big and at odds with its surroundings. It was a statement of creation by Nickson. A statement of his own importance maybe. I heard Toby say my name and hand the guard my passport.

I rang earlier, said Toby. I spoke to Dr. Bakircioglü. She said to come straight to her.

The guard nodded.

Main entrance. You are to be accompanied at all times. No wandering off into unauthorised space, you are to stay with Dr. Bakircioglü. Do you understand?

He spoke like a robot, his words solid and heavy. Toby nodded and took back my passport.

Got it, no wandering, stay with the Doc, he said.

The guard stepped back. He placed a finger to a small black earpiece. He spoke in a whisper. After a minute the gate began to slowly slide open. There was no sound, just a slow widening that reminded me of a snake's mouth opening, gaping, ready to swallow. When it was fully open, the guard waved us through.

We didn't speak. I could tell Toby wanted to say

something, anything, and at the same time I think he understood that he'd said enough already, that it wasn't his words I needed to hear now.

As we approached the pyramid, the blackness of it grew like a shadow desperate to block out the sun. When we got close I expected to see past the glass and into the interior of the building but the panels of the pyramid were opaque. Whatever was inside was hidden.

Toby slowed the Jensen to a stop. There were wide steps leading up to the main entrance. Each step was white marble, but their whiteness was dulled beneath the black peak above them. A short woman in a black suit was standing at the top of the steps, her arms folded seriously. She had short grey hair and wore those round glasses you only ever see sociopathic doctors wear in films.

Are you sure about this? said Toby.

I didn't want to answer him. I just nodded.

I need to hear you say it Leo, he said. I get it, you're angry. This is horrible, all of it is, but I love you, mate. I never wanted to hurt you. All I need to know is that this is what you want to happen. You want to go inside whatever this place is, and you want that woman to tell you whatever it is you need to know.

I nodded again. I wasn't looking at him. Outside the

main doors was another of the fallen eights, the snake eating itself. I don't know why but seeing that snake, watching it consuming its own tail, frozen, locked in the act, made me feel sick.

I want to do this, I said and before Toby could say anything else I opened the door and got out of the Jensen.

The woman watched me as I walked up the steps. I could see her small eyes studying me and what made it worse was that she tilted her head a little, just like Eadie, but there was no warm curiosity in that gesture. She was cold, too interested in the specifics of me. I almost felt like she was dissecting me with her gaze. I could hear Toby's feet on the steps behind me.

Mr. Roslin, she said in a loud voice that didn't match her stature. Her accent made the *r* of my name long, rolling. I am Dr. Bakircioglü. I understand you have some questions for us.

She was smiling, snake-like herself, her lips painted purple. I could see that the perfect white of her teeth was interrupted by the slight imperfection of a gap.

And you must be Mr. Saravakos, what a pleasure it is to have an artist in our facility. I'm afraid we'll all seem philistines to you, but I must reassure you, I have read much of your work and have found it very engaging.

Toby stood beside me. Thank you, he said. Though I'm sure what you do here is much more important than my poems.

She laughed. Not at all, Mr. Saravakos. Poetry is life and we are in the business of life are we not? Is that not why young Leo here has come to visit us? Is that right, Leo?

I went to speak but I could still feel her eyes studying me, piercing inside me.

Yeah, said Toby. That's about right, isn't it matey? Shall we go inside then?

I felt suddenly cold. There was no snow but the openness of the fields and the immensity of the pyramid above me, so huge and oppressive, made me suddenly shiver. There was a part of me that wanted to turn around and get back in the Jensen. To be ignorant. To make denial stretch forever.

Come, come then, Leo, said Dr. Bakircioglü. I'm sure you have many questions. I know Mr. Nickson is very keen to answer them.

Mr. Nickson, said Toby. I didn't think he'd be here. I mean I thought we were here to see you. Is he here?

She laughed again, the gap in her teeth making the laugh a little hiss.

If only, Mr. Saravakos, she said. Mr. Nickson is, I am afraid, on business in Singapore. He has however made time

190

in his schedule to speak to Leo because Leo is very special to Mr. Nickson. Now, come, it is much warmer inside.

Dr. Bakircioglü turned and as she stepped towards the black door it slid open and we followed her inside. With a woosh the door shut behind us. I looked up. We were standing in a huge atrium. There was no reception desk and not a single sign of any other workers The atrium was a semicircle and all around were white doors numbered from 1 to 25. The floor of the atrium was made of the same sheer white marble as the steps, and over the semicircular wall the words FORESIGHT NICKSON shone in pale white lights. The whole room was quiet, serene almost.

Follow me if you will, said Dr. Bakircioglü. Her heels tapped rhythmically over the marble as she moved quickly towards one of the doors. We followed. When she reached door 14, she tapped a keypad on the right-hand side. I expected the door to open and for us to step into a lift, but when it opened there was only a long corridor, the same white marble floor, the same black walls with white doors interspersed at equidistance all along to an end we couldn't see.

Would either of you like you a drink? she asked as we followed her along the corridor. Tea? Coffee? Water? Or would Leo like a Coca-Cola perhaps?

I'm fine, I said.

Very well, said Dr. Bakircioglü. I myself may have some water, I have a very intense day, many small issues to be dealt with. I must say, I was rather happy when I received your call, Mr. Saravakos. Leo is so very dear to all of us, I was delighted that you wanted to come in so urgently though obviously slightly concerned as to the reason for that urgency.

She stopped and turned to us. She was smiling but the smile looked awkward on her purple lips.

I do hope the matter is not too serious, she said.

Not at all, said Toby. Leo just wanted some things clarified.

The doctor nodded her head, looked from Toby then to me, all the while smiling.

Well, Leo, I'm sure we can clarify anything you need clarifying. As I have said, Mr. Nickson has made himself available for you because of how much we all care about you. Your concerns are our concerns. We are here, if I may be so bold, to serve you.

She touched a panel beside the door, tapped in a sequence of numbers, and this time when the door opened there was a lift.

Dr. Bakircioglü motioned for us to step inside.

I'm afraid I won't be joining you in your meeting with Mr. Nickson. This lift will take you to the Research Units. My secretary, Mr. Stonehouse, will show you to Mr. Nickson's private office.

She turned to me and put out a small hand. I noticed her fingernails were painted the same purple as her lips.

I wish you all the best, dear Leo, she said, her head tilting again.

Thank you, I said. When I took her hand, I expected her skin to be cold but if anything, her fingers were too warm, and she gripped my hand hard.

When she let go of my hand, she shook Toby's and with a curt nod she turned and walked back along the corridor. We stepped into the lift and Toby let out a sigh, slumping against the wall.

This place is something else, he said. Did you feel that woman's grip? Jesus, my dad didn't have that strong a grip.

The doors shut without either of us pressing any buttons. The same white glow that lit up the FORESIGHT NICKSON sign pulsed down from the ceiling of the lift. A low thrum filled the room and then we were moving up. There was no jolt, no feeling of being pulled up, it was much gentler than that.

Are you okay? said Toby.

I couldn't look at him, but the plain black walls meant there wasn't anywhere else to look.

I'm fine, I said. I just want to get this done.

I understand. Just remember I'm here.

I pushed myself against the wall. It was so black that I almost felt like if I pushed hard enough against it, the wall would become liquid and I could drown into it, vanish.

I wish you weren't here, I said and as soon as I spoke, I heard the cruelty in my words.

Roslin, he began to say but the lift came softly to a stop and the doors breathed open.

A tall man in a tight-fitting black suit and white collarless shirt was standing outside. He was a lot younger than Dr. Bakircioglü, but his smile had the same cold emptiness.

Welcome, said the man. I'm Stonehouse.

His head darted between us like a bird as he spoke.

Hello, Stonehouse, said Toby.

If you'll follow me, said Stonehouse, his head still darting, I'll show you to Mr. Nickson's offices.

Without waiting for us, Stonehouse turned and began walking away. The lift had brought us to an even longer corridor that stretched to our right and left. Stonehouse was heading away to our left, so we followed him. As we walked, I noticed there were no doors here but every few metres there were words just above head height. Research Bay 53. Ageing Unit 17. Fast Processing 7. Maturing Suite 42.

What do you do up here? I asked.

Stonehouse didn't stop walking. These are our research units, Leo. It's essentially where we try out new techniques in cloning. I'd very much like to show you exactly what goes on behind each door but I'm afraid even my clearance doesn't reach that high. Suffice to say, it's where all our great ideas were in a sense born.

The word *born* sounded wrong from his mouth. Too cold and unnatural. It felt like to Stonehouse the word had a different meaning.

Toby tapped me on my arm, and I looked towards him.

Bloody robot, he mouthed, smiling.

The corridor was so long that as we walked down its hollow length, I had the feeling again that I'd been separated, that some part of me was continuing to move beyond myself along the corridor and ahead of me, ahead of Toby and Stonehouse. Then there was another me who'd come to a complete standstill. It wasn't that I was refusing to move because I *was* moving. I was walking. It was that I felt like even the movements I was making, my legs in the act of walking, weren't real movements. I was still. Ahead of me that dead corridor stretched like an unnavigable river, so empty I could have drowned in the solidity of its space. But I moved. We all moved. I was walking beside Toby and there was no other me out ahead and I had not simply stopped. I was moving towards whatever end that silent tunnel led me to.

Eventually, the corridor came to an end. There was no sign to say what room we'd come to, but Stonehouse simply tapped once on the wall and the space ahead of us shot open.

If you'll come this way, I've taken the liberty of providing some refreshments for you both. Stonehouse stepped into the room, and we followed him.

There was nothing dark in that space. Every wall was white, as blank as a room could get. There were two white leather armchairs in the middle of the room and a low glass table ahead of them. There was a large flat-screen television on the far wall facing the chairs, but aside from that the room was completely bare. As I stepped inside the air felt different, cleaner. I heard Toby breathe in.

Whoa, he said. What do you do, pump in pure oxygen?

Stonehouse laughed. It was a small, uncomfortable laugh. Mr. Nickson does like his air to be as fresh as possible. Please, take a seat. Mr. Nickson will be joining you very soon.

196

We walked to the armchairs. The table had two glasses of water and two bottles of Coca-Cola set out.

Toby took a seat and reached for the water, but I kept standing, looking around the bare room. It was so plain, lifeless, that I had this feeling that I wouldn't find anything in here except for clean air. I wanted to leave.

Stonehouse stood in the doorway.

Is there anything else I can get for you? he asked.

I wanted to say, yes, you could show me the way out, you could tell me this is all a joke, that I'm as real as you, as real as Toby, that I don't need to ask any questions and I don't need answers, but I knew that was a lie.

No, I said. I'm fine.

Stonehouse smiled and stepped back.

I'll leave you to your meeting, gentlemen. I'll be waiting outside for you when you're done. Simply walk to this door and it will open for you. If you need anything at all, please simply say my name and I'll be right with you.

He smiled again and the door slid smoothly shut on him.

Toby sipped his water. This is crazy, he said. I don't think I've ever tasted water this pure. It doesn't even actually taste like water.

I crossed the room and sat in the other armchair.

I was about to tell him that I was scared. But before I

could speak, the television screen came on and a man was standing in front of a large writing desk. Behind him was an arched window and to one side there were bookshelves filled with what looked like old books.

If the man was Euros Nickson, then he must have been at least eighty, but he didn't look a day over forty. He was as tall as Stonehouse but beneath the dark grey suit and pristine white shirt he looked fit, muscular. He didn't have a grey hair on his head, his face cleanly shaven. As he stood, arms casually folded, smiling at us, he looked more like a Hollywood actor than a billionaire scientist.

Leo, he said, spreading his arms as if I were his grandchild, as if we knew each other. My God, boy, you look like a man. I'm so damn happy to see you, Leo, so damn happy.

Euros Nickson was British, but his accent was California-soaked just like his tanned skin.

And Toby Saravakos, what a pleasure, what a goddamn pleasure to have a poet of your talent in my humble office. Wow, I wish I was there to shake your hand.

We're very grateful to be here, Mr. Nickson, said Toby.

Nickson waved Toby's words away. Jesus, man, call me Euros. Let's keep this friendly, informal. Unless you're pitching for funding that is? Is that why you're here, Leo? You after a few dollars from me to get you going in life?

198

Nickson laughed. It was a loud, real laugh that made it almost feel like he was in the room with us.

No, I said, my voice flat. I don't want money. I just want answers.

Toby put his hand on my knee. What Leo means, Mr. Nickson, is that he just needs some reassurances.

Nickson let out a sigh like he was breathing out cigar smoke, and his huge hand rubbed at his chin as he nodded.

I see, I see. Well, Jesus, it's not like I didn't see this day coming. So come on Leo, shoot. I'll try to answer any question you ask as honestly as I can. If there's one thing you can rely on me for it's my honesty. I would never lie to you, Leo.

I don't know if it was the warmth of his tone or his brash demeanour, but I felt more relaxed than I'd felt in days. I felt my body ease back into the soft armchair.

Okay, I said. I had so many questions. They'd run through my mind, multiplying, adding to each other, building on each other, from the moment Toby had started telling me the truth. But as I sat in that room, I only cared about one thing, I only had one question.

What's wrong with me? I asked.

Nickson smiled. It was such a warm, grandfatherly smile. I wanted him to tell me there was nothing wrong with me or at least nothing he couldn't fix. He looked magnificent. He looked like the only man in the world who could make anything possible. I knew he could fix me.

He stroked his chin again and sighed. Ah, shit, kid, he said. I wish I could tell you a different story, but the truth is you just ran out of time. That's all, boy. You just ran right out of time.

Toby shot up. Now hang on. What the hell do you think you're doing saying that to him?

Nickson raised a hand. Sit down, Saravakos. It does no good lying to the boy now does it? Sit yourself down, man.

As if bidden by God, Toby sat down.

The grandfatherly look vanished from Nickson. He had grown suddenly stern, as cold as Dr. Bakircioglü. I understood then who Euros Nickson was. He was a man who made things that others couldn't. He was a man who built a pyramid in a Cheshire field so everyone knew he existed. He was a man who had made billions from giving the world the impossible. He wasn't a god, but right then as I sat in that armchair, I understood that he wanted to be a god and that to him I was nothing. I was just another experiment. There were no kind words coming. No promises. No fixes. No miracles.

You want the truth, is that right, Leo? he said.

I do, I said. I was gripping the armchair to stop my hands shaking.

And you can handle it can you?

I can, I said.

Nickson perched on the table. He looked at me, not in the way Dr. Bakircioglü had. He looked at me with pity.

Yeah, he said with a smile that almost spoke of pride in my bravery. More likely a pride that something he had created could be so brave. I know you can, he said. Okay, so let's start with these episodes you've been having. What do you think they are?

I shrugged. I don't know. Am I dying?

That's a very complex question. If I say yes, would that be the truth? If I say no, would I be lying? Now let's start at more simple point. Listen, Leo, do you know why I helped your dad?

Because you liked him, I said.

Nickson smiled. I do like the guy, I really do. But that isn't a reason to go breaking the law, is it? No, I helped your dad and your mum because doing that was helping myself. You passed all those rooms on the way in, didn't you?

The Research Units, said Toby.

That's right, said Nickson. That's all we do here. We research. We ask questions and we find answers. Sometimes we can't find answers, so we keep asking questions. You were a question, Leo. When I heard what happened to you it broke my heart, but I didn't get to where I am today by acting on emotion alone. I got to where I am by seeing an opportunity. Your parents were desperate and that meant they could be trusted. I made them an offer, I'd try to bring you back just as you were and in exchange, they'd let me keep all the data on you, log your progress, check up on you from time to time. You have to understand, Leo, I'm not a good man but that doesn't mean I'm a bad man. I'm just a man trying to do things others don't have the balls to do. I helped your mum and dad; I gave you back to them. Those rooms you passed; we made you there.

I glanced behind me but there was only the wall where the door had been. I remembered the names of the rooms. Ageing. Fast Processing. Maturing.

How many times? I asked.

Nickson laughed. You're a smart boy. Leo. We struggled, of course we did. It took us a hell of a while to get you stable, sometimes we just couldn't quite make you stable so we moved on, started again. At last, we got you to a point where we thought you were good.

Thought, I said.

Thought, he repeated. It's been nearly thirteen years, Leo.

That's a hell of a run. You've done better than even I could have expected. Do you realise what breakthroughs creating you has enabled? How many lives you've made better just by existing?

Toby's leg was shaking.

It's okay, I said, putting my hand on his leg. I understand. I'm failing then, it's true.

Nickson shrugged. It was nonchalant, disinterested.

That's an ugly word and not one I'd use, but yeah, you're failing. You see, the fact is, all these things happening to you, the blackouts, and neurological issues, they're clear signs of instability in your genetic foundations. Think of yourself as a structure built on those core foundations. Your DNA, the DNA we took from the first you, well that's your essential foundations, but they shouldn't be in you, I mean the you that's sat in that chair now, they don't actually belong to you. So maybe they're pushing you away, reacting, and as they do that, you're gradually destabilising.

What does that mean? I asked.

Nickson glanced at his watch. I told you, Leo. It's simple. It means you're out of time. That's all. You had a damn good run but it's the end of the road, kid.

And there's nothing you can do? said Toby.

Nickson pushed a hand through his hair. Sure, maybe. I

could bring Leo out to Tokyo. We could do work on him. Might mean starting again, cloning this Leo all over. Maybe that would work, maybe not. Thing I have to ask myself is what's in that for me? Do I want to bring you all the way out here and risk others knowing about you? Hell, maybe on some level it would be interesting to know why my product has failed.

Product, said Toby. He's not a product. He's alive, you prick.

Nickson laughed as if Toby had made a joke. Come on, give me a break, he said. I made the kid. I gave you back to your mum and dad, Leo. I gave you a life when by rights you shouldn't have had one.

Nickson paused. He moved his neck as if he had a crick in it, half closed his eyes.

There is one thing I'm a little curious about, he said, opening his eyes.

*You're* curious about? said Toby.

I touched my uncle's hand. It's okay, Toby. What are you curious about, Mr. Nickson?

Nickson leaned forward. Do you see anything?

I moved my hand from Toby's. What do you mean? I asked.

I mean do you ever see something, I don't know,

something that others might say isn't there? One of our clients in Qatar claimed he did, right towards the end. He claimed his visions were real, called them *living ghosts*. He even went as far as to claim these ghosts were trying to communicate through him. Of course, this was all part of his deterioration. Waking dreams, that was how my technicians explained what he was seeing. Fragments made up of his brain's slow failing and, of course, the poor bastard's own mental anxiety at what was happening to him. A kind of madness brought on by an awareness of one's self, too much awareness maybe. So, Leo, tell me, do you see things?

Would it make a difference if I did? I said.

He shrugged nonchalantly. Maybe. Maybe it'd make me more interested in your specific situation.

As I looked at Nickson, his eyes almost hungry for me to make him curious, I thought of the hawk, the runner, the past that I was being forced to see. *Living ghosts*. Recordings relayed just for me. I looked at him. He was smiling, watching me, studying me like I was some machine he wanted to take apart and understand but only if there was something in me worth understanding.

No, I said. I've never seen anything. I just get headaches, can't move and stuff. All that rubbish. I'm just sick.

Nickson nodded slowly. The spark of interest gone. A shame, he said, still smiling. A real shame.

He sat back and sighed. So come on, Leo. What do you want me to do here? You tell me what the hell you want me to do to make this better?

I swear I almost heard a slither of concern in his voice, as if he did care.

I want you to tell me how long? I said.

No, you don't, said Nickson. No one needs to know that.

I want to know, I said. You owe me that.

Nickson raised an eyebrow. I owe you? Is that what you think? Okay, Leo, I'll tell you. When's your birthday?

The twentieth of December, I said.

There you go, now you know, said Nickson. He glanced at his watch again.

What do you mean? I said. What does my birthday have to do with this?

Everything, he said though he sounded bored now. You died on your birthday. We brought you back at that exact age. The tests we did on you when your mum and dad brought you to NIX, they told us what we already knew. The rate at which you're deteriorating increases every day. All the models gave us one date. December twentieth. I'm sorry, I did try to warn you, kid.

The weight of his words felt like the whole pyramid was crashing down on me. December twentieth. Just days. Deteriorating. Failing. I was a product. I was out of time.

Nickson was talking. Toby was shouting. The door opened and Stonehouse came in flanked by two security guards in black suits. One of them grabbed Toby, he pushed her off. The television screen was black again. Nickson was gone. Toby pushed Stonehouse.

No! I shouted as the other security guard grabbed Toby by his arm. Stop, we'll go. Come on, Toby. Let's just go.

I pulled him away from the guards. We walked quickly down the hall towards the open lift. Stonehouse and the guards stayed with us as the lift descended. When the doors opened, I shot out ahead of everyone else. I was walking so fast that Stonehouse had to run past me to open the doors into the atrium. When we were back there it wasn't empty. It must have been the end of the day because workers were streaming out of the white doors, some in suits, others in lab coats. A few of them looked at me and I wondered if they'd seen photographs of me, my file, if they knew I was one of their failed products. I walked faster until we were outside. It was dark and colder. Toby's Jensen was parked where we'd left it. Toby got in and started the engine and as soon as I was in, he was racing back down the drive, hitting the speed bumps hard. The security gate was open, and we raced through that onto the long Cheshire roads.

Neither of us had anything to say. I closed my eyes but all I could see was Nickson's smug arrogance and I could hear his words. *You're out of time, that's all.* Time felt like it was racing away from me, slipping away from me. I wanted to tell Toby to stop, pull over, to run out into the field and be like the runner, make myself frozen, make myself stop. Nothing can deteriorate if it stops. Nothing can fail if there's no time moving it towards an end point. But I didn't tell Toby to stop, I just let him drive. I let the car's movement be the same as everything else, let it push me closer to that date. My use-by date. My birthday. My death day.

When we pulled up outside my house, I jumped out. Toby called to me, but I ignored him. I walked away from the house, but he didn't follow me. As I walked, I kept telling myself I wasn't real. I wasn't Leo. I was false. I was a lie. I was dying. I was failing. But I wouldn't let myself fail. I wouldn't just stagger towards the end that Nickson and his scientists had predetermined for me. I wouldn't curl up and wait to vanish. Why not feel life fully before the day came when I couldn't feel it anymore? December twentieth. My birthday. I even had a few days left. A handful of days to live. A handful of days to feel. A handful of days left to be the Leo Roslin I never really was.

So, I ran.

# Seventeen

I ran down High Street and didn't care how icy it was or think for a minute that I would slip, fall. I just ran. I must have looked strange to anyone passing. I wasn't wearing running gear, just the jeans and shirt I'd worn to Eadie's. But the more I ran, the faster I felt I was running. Light, as if there was no ground, just air beneath my feet. I was at the bottom of the hill before I knew it. I turned right, ran on the road itself because I didn't care what cars might come, and when they came, when they beeped at me, swerved, I didn't deviate from my path or step to the safety of the pavement. What did it matter if they ran me down? What would the *Northwich Guardian* say tomorrow? Dead boy killed again. Clone mown down. Why would anyone care? What was dead surely couldn't die again.

I ran and ran. Soon I was passing the Cock O'Budworth

and without any conscious thought I turned up towards Eadie's private school, turned off Belmont Lane up the little road to the old country house that was now the private school. The road was uneven, full of potholes, but even though my ankle went more than once, even though I fell, I just got right back up, kept running. There were sheep in the field. I couldn't see them, but I could hear them, and it felt like they were crying out at me as I passed. You count sheep in dreams. I counted the sheep I couldn't see. One, two, three. None of this was a dream. I ran on until I was in the deep dark of the grounds. I'd never been up to the school before, it had always just been there behind the hedges off the main road, a secret place that didn't concern me.

My heart was racing so I stopped, crouched, breathed in the icy air, looked up at the lightless school. I thought of Eadie in there learning about science, biology maybe. Maybe she'd learnt about clones. Did they teach that in school? I had no idea. I tried to think of my own school, remember what I was taught but I laughed then because of course there was nothing there to remember. Either it was gone, lost like all my dying memories, their half-lives too quickly deteriorating, or it had never been. Was that it? Had Mum and Dad never even sent me to school? Had they kept me hidden, a secret, illegal? The only child clone in the world, that's what Toby had said. I was a crime. I went against a UN convention. I was an abomination. I laughed again. I heard my laugh echo into the empty space around me. It was faint, fading.

I'm no one, I said.

There was no echo. I had barely whispered the words. Why hide anymore? Why couldn't everyone know what I was?

I made myself stand taller, raised my arms high like I was reaching for something in the night above.

I'm no one! I shouted, screamed at the old school building as if its crumbling stone was to blame.

My voice bounced off the walls. It echoed. It was copied. Repeated. *I'm no one*, it said. Fading, deteriorating. I had this flash of a memory then. I remembered Mum singing to me. *Little Sir Echo*. That didn't make sense. I knew the memory came from when I was very little, before I was five, but that couldn't be. I wasn't that Leo. As I stood in the Belmont grounds, I could hear her voice singing to me. *Little Sir Echo, how do you do? Hello, hello…* I could feel her finger tracing a little circle on my palm. I could remember falling asleep to her voice. *You're a nice little fellow, I can tell by your name, but you're always too far away, away.*

I ran.

I ran back down the potholed road but this time I jumped the holes. I was sprinting. I was impossible to stop. I ran back onto Belmont Lane, turned left towards the back end of Great Budworth. I ran and ran, faster and faster, until I was back in the village, my heart pounding, no breath left in my body. I wanted to keep running until whatever I was began falling away, bit by bit, piece by piece. Maybe if I ran long enough, I'd start to disintegrate, literally fall apart, and all of my pieces would be scattered about Cheshire for no one to find. Buried by snow. Forgotten. I'd be okay with that; I'd accept that fate.

But I was exhausted. My body would no longer let me keep going. I was back near the pub, the church over to my left. I leant against a lamppost, breathed, tried to make my heart slow. I was sweating and the sweat that rolled down my face was like little rivers of ice.

I knew Becca was there before I saw her.

I'd closed my eyes. I was close to tears because I was thinking about the weight of what Toby had told me. I wasn't me. I wasn't Leo. But even with my eyes closed I knew she was there.

When I opened them, I saw Becca walking up the road back out of Great Budworth. She was foggy, faint, a wisp of a person. Every now and again she would vanish then reappear. Just as she was nearly out of sight, she turned back and I swear she looked at me and her head tilted, almost the way Eadie's does, and I knew she wanted me to follow her.

Did it matter if she wasn't real? Did it matter if my brain was so lost in its own dissolution that it was creating these images and mirages? I followed her.

It's crazy but I kept my distance. Why did I do that? She wasn't real, she couldn't turn around and ask me why I was following her. She would never see me but even knowing that I still followed her slowly.

Every now and again she did look back, but I knew she wasn't looking for me. She was scared. I could see that in her eyes. She'd been crying, her mascara streaked. She had a short fur coat on, a dress underneath and boots. She didn't seem as young as the first time I saw her, but I could tell that was only an effort at looking older. She was still just a girl.

She walked up Westage Lane and turned on to Heath Lane. There was a house up on the left and she turned into its drive, looking back one more time.

A light came on. I think it was the light from a phone's torch. It came from the drive. A man came forward, he had a thick black beard, and his head was shaved. He was much older than Becca, too old, but she went straight to him and standing on her tiptoes she kissed him. At first, he seemed to allow the kiss but then he pushed her away, a little too roughly so she almost stumbled back on the shale drive. She went to him again, but he pushed her. This time she did fall but he caught her by her wrists and as he caught her, I saw the bracelet she'd been wearing snap, fall unnoticed from her arm to the shale. I saw her lips move. I couldn't hear what she said. He shook his head, waved his arms. He was shouting at her. She went to him, almost threw herself at him, put her arms around him desperately. She was speaking again, the same word over and over. He seemed to relent a little, his body relaxing as he held her back. They spoke. I stood there watching my ghosts, wondering what secret words were passing between them, what promises or lies. She nodded and he took her hand and together they walked up the drive. I followed, quicker now, the pretence that they might see me abandoned. The light of the phone died. At the end of the drive was a garage. I saw the man open the garage door and push Becca inside. I saw him look back. He looked right at me. I saw his eyes. I believe he saw me. When he shut the door I expected this vision, this evidence of my damaged brain, to end, but instead there was a flickering and the garage door opened. The man came out alone, but he wasn't wearing the same clothes as when he'd gone inside. This time he was only in his dressing gown and slippers. He was looking up to his house as if he was nervous of being seen. I watched as he hurried down the drive, scanning the shale. I knew what he was looking for. I could see him getting more panicked, kicking at the shale, bending, picking something up, throwing it away, and then something caught his eye and he grabbed at the ground. When he stood, he was holding the bracelet. I saw him smile then. It wasn't a happy smile, a nice smile. It was sick. It was cruel. He was sick. He was cruel.

In that moment, seeing that ghost holding Becca's bracelet, I knew what had happened to Eadie's sister, and I knew too that I had to tell her. It didn't matter if all I'd seen was created from glitches in my mind. I'd seen Becca in the graveyard. I'd seen her dropping her ring and I'd found that ring. That glitch, the memory that wasn't my own, was real somehow. It had happened and though I had no answer to why my mind would be seeing a memory I never lived, I knew what memory I was being shown. I hadn't been able to see inside the garage, but I'd seen Becca go in and I hadn't seen her come out. It was clear to me what I was being shown.

# *Eighteen*

All I could do was tell Eadie.

I walked in a trance back into Great Budworth. Nickson's words were too big, too impossible, for me to escape. They swam around my mind as I walked. I think I tried to kill them with memories. I know how ridiculous it was, but as I walked, I tried to see myself as a baby, as a toddler, as a four-year-old. I tried to see myself running alongside the river, see Rabalon falling from my grasp, see myself reaching for my bunny then toppling into the water, feel the ice crack as my body's weight shattered the frozen surface, feel the freezing water shock my little body then the immediate numbing, the fall into the dark then the deeper fall into the deeper dark. I tried to imagine if I'd fought, swum. Could I even swim then? I could only see myself falling deeper and deeper as if the river were an ocean and the more I floated down to its depth the darker everything got until there was only black, then numbness, and a feeling of being too far away from anywhere and anyone to ever go back. But none of that was real, was it? None of it was an actual memory. I couldn't possibly remember that moment. I'd never lived it. It wasn't my moment to recall. My memories only began six months after Leo drowned, when they brought me out of whatever tank they made me in. What did the scientists do to wake me? Inject me with something to shock me into life? Have Mum hold me until I woke, and she could say, shush, it was only a dream, you were only asleep? I hate lies.

I came to Eadie's path. There was no car parked out front, no lights on downstairs. I looked up to her bedroom and saw her light was on. I thought about finding a stone, throwing it at her window. That's what forbidden lovers do in films isn't it? Then the girl would come to the window, put a finger over her lips and beckon the boy to climb the trellis into her arms. But I didn't have to throw a stone. As I was scanning the pavement, I heard a light knocking, and looking up saw Eadie standing at her window. She tilted her head. She had her coat on and a woolly hat. I half-waved up to her and as I did, she mouthed something then pointed across to the pub car park, mouthed something again and held up a finger that I'm sure meant give me a minute.

I thought about going home, not waiting for her in the car park. I felt like a fraud. How could I meet her, speak to her, when I wasn't the person she thought I was? The person I thought I'd been. That was a lie, wasn't it? To meet her and pretend to be Leo when I knew what I really was. And then there was the bigger lie. The one I'd tried to escape from on my run, that one devastating thought that I'd known was there as I walked back into the village but refused to see. Let's call it the truth. I was dying. If Nickson was right, I had just days left in this world. Wasn't it cruel for me to meet her? To let her think she might get to know me, that we might have more moments like this. It would be better if I'd just walked away, went home, shut myself in my room and waited for December twentieth. My birthday. My last day. Better if she forgot about Leo Roslin just as she'd never known I existed until a few days ago.

I didn't go home. I crossed the empty road to the pub. It was nearly last orders and there weren't many cars parked up. At the far end of the car park there was a low wooden fence, so I walked to that and, scooping snow away, sat there and waited.

Her one minute was more like ten. As I waited, I looked

up into the night. The sky was clear and away from the street lamps' harsh intrusion, I could see the immensity of the stars. It's strange with stars how you look up, don't notice them, and then all of a sudden you see one and after that you see them all, can't help but see them. I wish I knew the names of constellations, at least then I could have pretended I understood something about the world, the universe. I could have said those stars above me were Orion's Belt and know for certain they were Orion's Belt. I could have said that the bright star was Sirius and know that meant the Dog Star and wonder why it was so much brighter than all the others. As I looked up at the stars, I had this crazy thought that my hawk was up there too. That if I looked hard enough, willed it to be there, it would come swooping down from the stars, hover above me until its wings slowed, its movement subsided and it became still. I would watch my hawk and understand why it was still. I think I understood. It was unmoving, frozen, because I was moving towards that same point of stillness. The runner, the hawk, maybe they were projections of what awaited me. Soon I would be like the runner and the hawk. I would stop moving. I would become still. I would look like a boy, but I would never be a boy again. Never be a man. I would be stuck in that point of time that was my eighteenth birthday forever just as the runner was stuck in the act of running and the hawk in the single act of hunting. We were the same and I wanted so much to see my hawk right then.

It never came.

Eadie came. She ran towards me and before I could say anything she threw herself into me, so I had no choice but to hold her. Then she kissed me. She kissed me hard as she had in her bedroom. I could only kiss her back.

Time doesn't matter in moments like that. I think they exist within their own little bubbles. Singularities. Isolated events. That kiss might have lasted a second or millennia. The world might have shifted as her lips joined with mine. Land masses shattered. Continents colliding and parting. Civilisations rising and falling. The sun shrinking, dying, expanding. There was only that kiss.

When she pulled away, I knew I had to tell her about Becca. Forget how crazy it might sound that I knew what I knew, just tell her. I swear I was ready to do that, but as always she was quicker than me, the first to act.

I went to his house today, she said, excited, her hands holding mine.

Whose house?

She put her head on my chest.

It's cold isn't it, she said. I wish I could just sleep till summer, don't you? Hibernate like a bear, then wake up when everything wasn't so ugly.

Eadie, I said, squeezing her hands. Whose house?

Oh, I thought you'd remember. I went to Prendergast's. He did it didn't he. Of course, he did, the ring you found is proof. You know he used to do odd jobs round the church, tidy the graveyard and creepy stuff like that. I don't think he dug graves because they're all really old, but he was here every day. When you found the ring, I just knew it was proof. Why else would it be in the graveyard? He'd left it there hoping Dad would find it one day, hadn't he? Like some kind of sick trophy right in front of us. I think he wanted us to find it just like you found it so we'd know someone had left it there. That's really horrible isn't it? But he's horrible like that, I can see it in his eyes. That's why I went to his house.

When? I said.

She looked up at me. It was right after all that stuff with you and Dad. I'm sorry that happened to you. He can be such a prick at times, I really hate him when he's like that. I'm sorry, I didn't even ask if you were okay. I was worried, I really was, but I saw someone helping you back to your house and Dad made me stay in my room all day. He's had to go to see some dying parishioner or something, I'm sure

222

he wouldn't have left me if he didn't have to. He probably thinks you'll come right back over and molest me, he doesn't understand anything.

She was talking so fast, like a bullet train speeding along the tracks without stopping until it reaches its destination no matter if anyone gets on or off.

Why would you go to his house? I said, managing to break into her words.

I had to, she said. I mean if he did hurt Becca, and I know he did, then there'd be something there wouldn't there? He kept the ring, so God knows what else he kept. I was very brave at first, I planned to just go right up and bang on his door, force him to tell me he did it.

That was crazy, I said. He might have hurt you.

Oh, I'd have called the police I think, or maybe not. I don't know, I didn't care, I just needed to know what he'd done. But when I got there, he was coming out with that ratty dog of his so I hid in the bus shelter. He lives down by that ghastly factory, do you know it? The one that looks like hell. I don't know how anyone could live there. Well, I saw him come out carrying a suitcase like he was going away somewhere. He gets in his crappy car, drives off, and I think, right, I need to break in, but I'm a complete coward really. I suddenly got scared. That's stupid, isn't it? I was right there, right outside his house and I could have smashed a window, found something, anything. But you know what I did? A bus was coming up the road, so I ran across to the other bus stop and I got right on that bus and came home. I'm a fraud, I know it. I promised myself I'd find something, prove Becca was hurt, but when I had the opportunity, I ran away like a little scared girl. I hated myself so much when I got home, then I look out my window and you're right there. I knew what we had to do right away.

Who?

I could feel her shaking with excitement as she spoke.

We, she said. Me and you, Weirdo.

I couldn't let her keep going with the lies she was telling herself. The factory was nowhere near the house I'd seen on Heath Lane. The man I'd seen didn't have a dog. She was wrong.

We can't, I said but she tugged on my hands.

Don't say that, she said. Please don't. You don't understand how much I need this. I can't let Becca down again. Please, Leo, I just want you to do one bad thing for me. Please say you'll be a criminal for me just for tonight. Please say you'll break into that monster's house with me and help me find something, anything, that proves he did it. Please, Leo, please.

I knew she was wrong. I should have told her she was wrong. I should have taken her right then and there to the house on Heath Lane, taken her to the garage. If there was any proof of what had happened to Becca, then maybe that proof was still in there. Four years wasn't too long. Maybe the bracelet I'd seen fall from her hands, the one I'd seen the bearded man take, was still in there too. Maybe even the bearded man was still in that house. I should have told Eadie, made her understand how wrong she was. But how could I tell her any of that? To even begin to tell her the truth I would have had to tell her that bigger truth, the one I'd only just found out. That I was a mess, a fake person seeing impossible visions. Ask her to believe in one of those visions and trust me that my vision was any more real than the story she'd been telling herself for years.

Okay, I said. Let's do it.

I knew you'd believe me, I knew it, she said, throwing her arms around me again and kissing me.

I let her kiss me, but I didn't kiss her back. Whatever she felt right then she was wrong, I didn't deserve her kiss. I was the fraud. I was made of nothing but lies.

# *Nineteen*

I took Toby's car. His keys were by the front door, and he was cooking in the kitchen, music loud, so I don't think he noticed. I lied to Eadie. It was easy to do after all the other lies I'd told or been told that day. I told her I had a licence, that it was my car.

We drove out of the village and turned left towards Northwich. She talked on the way about Prendergast. How everyone knew he was a pervert. That his wife had left him when she found out, that he hadn't seen his kids for years, that there were rumours he'd been in prison before he came to Cheshire, but her dad had told her that everyone deserves a second chance, that he wouldn't listen to any accusation against Prendergast even after Becca vanished. She told me her dad blamed Becca and Becca alone. Becca had let herself down. Becca had failed herself. Becca had run away because she thought the grass was greener on the other side. Why hadn't he looked for her? That's what Eadie couldn't understand. How could a parent just switch off from a child like that, no matter how a child had changed or let them down? Surely when you had a child you made a promise to always be there for them no matter what. I thought of my own parents. Is that what they'd thought they were doing? Protecting me by bringing me back? Being there for me by giving me a chance to live again? I imagined Mum when she was told about my drowning. Had she collapsed into a heap on the floor? Had she screamed? Had she been lost for all those months without me so when Euros Nickson gave her that glimmer of hope, had she done what any grieving parent would have done when given the chance to be with their child again? Eadie said her dad wasn't a bad man, he was a good father. She knew how angry he could get, how severe he seemed. He didn't mean what he'd said to me, he was just scared, that's what she thought, scared of losing another daughter, scared of his only child being led astray. I said I wasn't capable of leading her astray and she said she knew that, that she was sure her dad knew that, but could I blame him for being so scared? That maybe he hadn't given up on Becca, not really, maybe he'd had to harden himself, accept a reality that his daughter had chosen a life without him. I thought of Dad. That sounded like how he would have coped with what happened to me. Hardened himself. Bricked himself up in a wall no one could bring down. And then I returned, his dead son brought back to life. Was that why he never really showed me love? Why he never held me, hugged me? It wasn't just that he was a tough man, a man's man who didn't believe in emotion. His wall had remained up because I wasn't his real son. Did he see me as an imposter who he had to force himself to love? There are fairy tales like that aren't there, ones about fairies taking babies and replacing them with cuckoo fakes, tricking the family into nurturing the child, loving them, while the real child is trapped in the fairy realm. Lies and love all intermingling in a mess. I was a cuckoo child. The real me was in a fairy realm he could never come back from.

Eadie told me she needed to do this. It wasn't for her, not really, it was for her dad. So he could see the truth, so he could let go and stop hating this imagined Becca and accept she'd never abandoned him, never run away, that she was taken away and if she could have come back she would have because she loved them, loved them all, that how she'd acted, what she'd said, wasn't the real Becca. The real Becca was her father's daughter, and she needed her dad now, needed Eadie too, needed them to uncover what Prendergast had done, free her, release her from the limbo she'd been in for four years.

That's all I want, she told me, for us to live and remember her, to know she loved us and that none of this was her fault. She didn't choose to leave us.

We reached Prendergast's house. It was a single, grey cottage standing alone opposite the chemical plant. I parked further down the street outside a row of terraces.

Did you see? His car wasn't there, said Eadie. I knew it. He's gone away somewhere. We'll have loads of time.

I turned off the engine. We have to get in the place first, I said. This isn't something I do all the time so I'd rather we get it done as quickly as possible.

Me neither, she said. But look, there's no one around. We can just go to the back of his house, break a window or something. You don't feel bad do you? He deserves this. He did it, Leo, I know he did, and I know you know he did. Come on, let's just get inside.

She moved to open the passenger door, but I put my hand on hers.

I'll go, I said. Even if he's not there, it's still dangerous. You stay here and if I find something I'll bring it to you, then we can call the police.

She frowned. Are you being a hero on me, Leo? Trying

to protect the frightened girl? That's not very attractive, you know.

I'm not doing that. It just doesn't need two of us to do this. You stay and look out for him.

He's not coming back, she said angrily.

He might. I'm not arguing about this, Eadie. If we're going to do this then this is the only way.

I've never been a forceful person, but I think it was the guilt of the lie, of letting her go on believing we'd find something. The only way I could protect her was by doing this myself.

You win, she said. You can be the hero burglar and I'll be your look-out even though he won't come back. Try not to leave me in here for hours. Do you realise how cold old cars are?

I'll be quick, I said.

Anything, she said. I don't care whether you think it might be evidence or not, if you find anything that even remotely looks like it might be something then take it, Leo. There has to be something, I know it.

I told her I would. That if there was even a scrap of evidence, even if it didn't look like it might be important, I'd take it. I knew there wouldn't be anything, but I had to keep lying.

I didn't run to Prendergast's. There was no one on the street and only a couple of cars whizzed by as I walked. On the right side of his house was a drive, overgrown with weeds, and a garage with rusted roller shutters that didn't meet the floor. The garage looked unlocked. I kept walking. On the other side of the house was some waste land full of broken bricks and a green wheelbarrow that was full of stagnant water. I glanced around. The road was empty, only a few lights shone in the factory. There was no fence around this side of the house, so I slipped into the waste land and went around the back of the house. I picked up a brick as I went. When I got to the back there was only a small window that was frosted like a bathroom window and then a back door. There was no window in the door and the bathroom window would have been too small for me to fit through. Part of me was relieved. I could have just walked away, told Eadie it was impossible, we could have driven back to Great Budworth. Maybe I could have told her the truth then. Not all of it, just the part she needed to hear. The bracelet, the bearded man, the garage. I could have told her that and then left her with the knowledge. I could have gone home to Toby and told another lie. Told him I was ready. That I understood. That it was all okay. But for some reason my hand was on the back-door handle and

231

when I pushed it down it didn't refuse to move. The door was unlocked.

I opened the door. A smell of old bin and blocked drains hit me. It was dark inside, so I switched on my phone's torch. I stepped into the kitchen and the smell got stronger. I shone the torch around the tiny kitchen. There was newspaper all over the floor and another smell of dog piss hit my nose as I walked further inside. There were empty beer cans scattered on the newspaper and discarded in the sink. A faint stink of tobacco mixed with the other smells. There was no door between the kitchen and the next room, so I walked through. That room wasn't really much of a living room. There was a tattered, bitten-at dog bed underneath the window. The curtains were brown, heavy with cobwebs and years of dirt. There was one armchair, no couches. The television was on a small coffee table. There were no pictures or photographs, no ornaments. No sign that this was a home that meant anything to anyone. More than that, there was clearly nothing in the room that didn't belong to a lonely drunk. No evidence of Becca. I could have turned around then. I'd done what Eadie had asked, gone through with it. I knew that searching anymore would bring the same result. Nothing. I could have just gone back the way I'd come in and told her Prendergast was innocent, she was wrong. But I knew she'd pester me to keep looking, tell me I hadn't looked properly, try to go in herself and do the search her way. I had no choice but to keep the pretence of a search up for a little while longer.

The stairs were uncarpeted, just bare wood with exposed nails and staples, splashes of paint here and there. The wallpaper was peeling. In the dim light of my torch, I saw damp stains and black mould speckling the wall. The stairs creaked as I climbed them, so I found myself going slower, until I remembered there was no one else in the house. Quickly, I reached the landing. There was a bathroom with a bath full of unwashed towels and a half-blocked toilet. A single beer can floated in the sink. I moved into the only bedroom. There were thin net curtains, brown and grubby, and the bed had no sheets or duvet, just a bare mattress with one yellowed pillow. The whole room stank of dog. I stood, shining my torch around, but just like the living room there was nothing in the room apart from the obvious. The only addition was a slim, wonky wardrobe beside the bed. I went to the wardrobe and when I opened a door the thing leaned even more, threatening to fall. I steadied the wardrobe, shined my torch inside. There were two checked shirts hanging up and a pair of old Levi's. On the bottom of the wardrobe were some magazines. I've never seen pornography.

I didn't think people still bought porn mags, but the bottom of Prendergast's wardrobe was strewn with them. I knelt, shone my torch on the magazines. They all showed similar images. Women pretending to be young. Women dressed as schoolgirls. Women in pigtails. Women in knee-high socks and undersized nighties. Women trying to look innocent even though they were naked. I picked one up. Its pages were crinkled and now I saw it closer the magazine looked old, the women's hair big and white-blonde. I turned the front page. A woman in a bonnet sat sucking a dummy. I threw the magazine back down. I suppose that could have been evidence that Prendergast was interested in young girls, but what good would it have really done to take them to Eadie? Doing that would have only embedded the lie in her head. The magazines were proof of nothing other than the fact that Prendergast was a pervert, a sick man with sick tastes, living alone in a pigsty, wasting his life in his own stink. I'd had enough of being in that environment. I slammed the wardrobe door.

Alright there, mucker, said a voice.

I jumped, turned, dropping my mobile.

The bedroom light came on. A dog snarled.

There was a man standing in the doorway. He had a thick black beard, scruffy, and he was wearing a long

Man Utd coat. At his side was a skinny Patterdale, its teeth bared.

Find anything interesting there, lad? said Prendergast, smirking.

I didn't even try to answer. I ran right at him, barged past him. I felt the dog snap at my leg, but I must have caught Prendergast off guard, because I was halfway down the stairs before I heard him pounding after me. He shouted something. The dog was barking. I kept running. The front door was open, so I ran straight outside. To my left was the Jensen but I knew I couldn't let him see me in that or see Eadie was with me. I heard Prendergast shout again, so I darted right and pelted into the waste ground. I'm not a fast runner but I hoped a man who lived his life like Prendergast was even slower. I was wrong. After barely a few yards, I glanced back and saw he was right on me, the little dog on its lead running with him, snapping and yapping.

I should have been paying more attention to where I was running. It was pitch black when I ran into the waste land, so I didn't see the river or even think there would be one.

Toby said I'd gone into the river before they'd had a chance to save me. One minute I was there, the next I'd vanished into the river. As I ran from Prendergast it was the same. One minute there was snow beneath my feet

235

and the next only air, then I was crashing through ice, biting-cold water in my mouth, covering me, weighing me down, as if it knew I'd escaped its intent once before and now it had got me again and this time it wasn't going to let go. I splashed around, shouted for help. I head the dog barking. I think I must have gone under the water because I remember punching at ice but it wouldn't break. There was only darkness. I'd never been so afraid. I had this flash of five-year-old me, how scared he must have been, how there had been the darkness for him and nothing else. I fought then, kicked, tried wildly to swim up to wherever the surface might be but pushed against ice, felt it shatter and then I was up, and I could breathe but my body was numb. I couldn't move my arms or legs. I was shaking uncontrollably. I heard someone shouting, a distant bark. I think I called out to Eadie, but she was unaware of any of this, safe in the Jensen waiting for me to come back to her with the evidence to convict Prendergast, evidence that didn't exist.

I tried to drag myself to the bank. Or at least in my mind that's what I was doing. I wasn't moving. My body was locked. I was on my back and even though I wanted to swim, to live, my body had given up. I didn't float back down into the water. I wasn't dragged beneath. The river didn't claim my debt. I simply lay there, floating on the surface and maybe my lack of motion, my rigidity, saved me. I thought for a moment I was staring up at the night sky but where were all the stars? There was only utter blackness. I understood then. I wasn't looking into the night. I was locked within myself, blacked out, trapped. My physical body was floating upon the water, but I was somewhere else where no one could reach me. Not death, I wasn't there yet. I was the runner upon the field. I was the hawk transfixed. I was frozen.

# *Twenty*

Stuck on a loop, the barking could have been going on forever. It was high-pitched, ear-popping. The bark of a small dog.

I felt like I was trapped in a room with just that dog, no doors, no means of escape. Just the piercing yelps bouncing off every wall like bullets through my eardrums.

I haven't had many hangovers in my life, but when I opened my eyes, I felt like I was living the worst hangover imaginable. My tongue was heavy, dry, and when I tried to lift my head, it seemed my skull was being crushed from the temples inwards. I lay back. Everything was blurry. My half-open eyes perceived only a fog. I was aware of movement, someone whistling, a tap running and of course the dog's monotonous bark.

Shut up, I said, my voice slurring as if I really had

drunk too much. I remembered the water, the darkness, the drowning.

I'll let a lot go, but I won't stand for that, said a gruff, gravelly voice. No one speaks to Jessy like that. You might want to thank her; I'd have let you drown if she'd quit yapping. Bloody tugging at my ankles she was. Had no choice but to drag you out just to shut the bitch up.

I turned my head. The fog was lifting but the crushing remained. I brought a hand to my head, pushed the ball of my palm against my skull.

Hurts does it? said the voice. Aye, near drownin'll do that. Drink this, can't say it'll take away the pain, but it'll warm you at least.

A shape came closer. A cup was pushed my way. I took it with unsteady hands, the ceramic scorching hot. I peered into the cup, expecting to see tea or coffee but a waft of beef filled my nostrils. The dog barked and I realised it was on the floor beside me, yelping up at me.

Bovril, said the voice.

My vision was clearing. I could see a thick beard, ruddy cheeks and overgrown eyebrows, unwashed and wild hair.

Prendergast, I said. The dog jumped up onto my chest, making the Bovril slop from my cup. The Patterdale clambered up my body, pushed its nose close to my face and sniffed, then licked my eye. Its breath smelt of tuna. I sat up, pushing a blanket away from my body. The dog jumped away at my movement. As soon as the blanket was gone, I realised I was naked.

All you bloody kids seem to know my name round here, he said. Can't say I like that situation much.

Where are my clothes? I said, still groggy. Where have you brought me?

I heard a lighter flick, smelt tobacco. Well, hark you now, that's frigging nice isn't it, he said. I save your life and you wake up asking stupid questions. Not a thank-you in sight. What do you think of that Jessy?

The Patterdale barked, the sound needling my ears.

I grabbed the blanket, brought it up to cover myself. My eyes were narrow, but I could see Prendergast more clearly. He was perched on the windowsill, cigarette in one hand, mug of Bovril in the other.

I didn't mean… I started to say.

Didn't mean to break into this place? cut in Prendergast. Didn't mean to near get yourself drowned? Bit of a mess you're in isn't it. Suppose I should call the police now you're awake, let them buggers deal with you.

I don't know if he expected me to react, to beg him not to call the police, but the threat sparked nothing in me.

What could the police do to me? Lock me in a cell for the few remaining days of my life? You can't give a sentence to someone if they've already received the worst sentence possible.

I thought... My tongue struggled to form words. I mean... I thought you were away. I didn't think...

I see, didn't think you'd be caught. What was it? You been watching me? Christ, lad, what on God's earth did you think I had in this shithole that was worth you spying on me? Hardly a mansion is it? What were you even looking for?

He sipped his Bovril, the Patterdale sitting at his feet, staring loyally up.

I looked at my own Bovril. It was almost black. I brought the mug to my lips but the intense beef smell made my stomach lurch.

Too rich for you, is it? he said. Bloody ironic that if you ask me. Look at you, more of a flat-white kid is that it? Sorry my tastes aren't so bloody refined.

I'm sorry, I said, glancing to the door. It was shut. I saw Prendergast look too.

Thinking of making a dart for it? he said. I'd maybe wait for your undies to dry first. You'll get yourself arrested running down the bloody street stark bollock naked.

Wouldn't want that would we? What would Mummy and Daddy say?

I groaned, the crushing pain in my head not subsiding. I'm sorry, I said. I was just…

Just a bloody idiot, is that it? Don't go having a heart attack now, I'm not calling no police, can't be arsed with all that faff. Seems to me you must have been pretty desperate to break in here. I get that, I can see it in your eyes. Whatever mess you're in must be bad to bring you round my way. Christ, it were a bad mess brought me here in the first place.

I rubbed at my eyes. My clothes weren't in the living room, and he was right, I don't think I would have got far running through Northwich naked in the middle of the night.

Thank you, I managed to say.

Thank me? he said, laughing. Thank Jessy more like. Bloody little hero she is. Too good for me, aren't you lass? How'd a man like me end up with such a good girl like you?

He leant down, scratched the dog lovingly behind her ears and she whimpered happily.

I can tell a hopeless case when I see one, he said, giving Jessy one last scratch. Wouldn't want to make shit worse for you. I've been in enough holes myself to know it doesn't help if other folk keep digging them for you. Want my advice?

Walk. Walk as much as you can and as far as you can. If that means you never stop walking, then so be it. Get as far away from other people and find a place to forget it all, whatever that all is. How about something stronger than Bovril?

He crossed the room, bringing the stench of unwashed clothes and ingrained tobacco with him, took my cup and went into the kitchen, whistling as he did. When he came back, he passed me the same cup but there was no Bovril, just a golden liquid.

It's cheap stuff, he said. Aldi's best whisky. Tastes like piss but does the job.

I hate whisky but my head was banging, and I was shivering a little. I put the cup to my lips, drank the whisky in one. The cup still smelt of beef, but the whisky was warm. I felt that warmth coat my throat and fill my body, a little furnace inside me.

That's the trick, he said, draining his own cup. So, not trying to ruin your night anymore, but that Sproston girl, she pissed off and left you.

I jumped up, clinging to the thin blanket. Where is she? Did you hurt her?

He laughed, looked into his cup as if there might be a few drops of whisky left and then, disappointed, dropped the mug to the carpet.

I waste the last of my best Scotch on you and in your next breath you go accusing me of hurting a girl? How's that for gratitude, Jessy?

Jessy was lapping at the mug, her tongue pushing inside for remnant whisky.

I didn't mean that, I said, the blanket barely covering my lower half. I know you're not… that you didn't…

Didn't hurt the other one. What were her name? Becky. Becca. Is that why you're here is it? She were pretty alright, can't say I didn't fancy her. Might have thought about doing something if truth's to be told and no one else is here to hear that. But she had better offers than me, mark my words. Blokes what could give her nice things, spend their money on her. What's it been, four years? The police asked me questions back then, course they did, but I was never a bloody suspect. How could I be? The girl just buggered off; everyone knew that. And did they ask that Ed Bray any questions? Did they bugger. He was always sniffing round that girl, even I could see that. But oh, Ed Bray, he were respectable, he were a big-shot lecturer up in Manchester, a family man. He wouldn't go round having wrong thoughts about a girl young enough to be his daughter would he? And then what was I? A monster right in their midst.

Why didn't you tell anyone you saw him with her? I asked.

He took a drag on his cigarette, tapped the ash to the carpet. Why should I? Why would I want to go crucifying some other poor bastard just because he'd had his head turned? What if he'd done nothing wrong apart from let his pecker do his thinking? Maybe I should've said something, but I couldn't be arsed. I didn't even tell that pompous bloody priest. Oh, I would've loved to see his face, I would've. Loved to have told him what Ed Bray was up to with his little princess. Nah, they can all think what they want, even now. Is that why you and her little sister came sniffing round? Do you think I'm a monster?

I looked to the door. There was a chain across it. I thought about the back door, but Prendergast was a bigger man than I'd thought he was. Maybe he'd be slow, maybe I'd be quicker, but there was no way of me knowing if the back door was locked just the same as the front.

I don't think you did anything, I said.

He was mid drag on his cigarette, stopped, brought the cigarette away, an eyebrow raised. Is that right? he said.

I know you didn't, I said.

He pointed the cigarette at me. And what bloody good does that do me? Do you know what I am, lad?

He paused, waited for me to answer but I didn't know what to say. A mess. A drunk. A nobody.

I'm what happens when you don't know how good you've got it, he said. I had a family me, a bloody wife, three kids. I had a house, a mortgage, a life. And what did I do? I killed it. I couldn't stop thinking with my whatsit, couldn't keep certain thoughts out of my head. Sick thoughts, that's what they were, I know that now, but it's too late isn't it. I made the mistakes, I let the thoughts turn into actions. I'm a bloody monster alright, just not for the reasons most people think. I'm a monster because I did this to myself, put myself here in this place with no way out. Do as I say, walk away. That's what you should do. Don't get tangled in nothing you can't untangle yourself from. Make the right choices when you can. Just walk away and don't stop walking until the thing that's pulling you down, the thing that'll kill you, is so far behind you it can never find you. You were lucky tonight, lad. I didn't have to pull you from that water. No one knew I was there; I could have just watched you drown and walked away. Well, I didn't, I'm a sodding saint I am. I've pulled you out, given you the chance I didn't have.

As he talked, stabbing the cigarette towards me, his voice fractured. I suddenly realised he was drunk. I saw a change come over him then. Bits of white foam formed as he spat the words.

So come on, he shouted. Get up, get your arse dressed and get the fuck out of my house.

He went out into the hall. When he came back he had my clothes, still soaking wet, scrunched up. He threw them at me. Jessy barked.

Shut it, he snapped, kicking at the dog, cigarette between his teeth. His eyes were suddenly wide, his eyelids twitching.

Didn't you hear me? Get up. Get out of my house. Go on. Get dressed or I'll throw you out on the street stark bollock naked.

I tossed the blanket aside, pulled on the wet jeans without bothering to look for my boxers, put my shirt on. My shoes were sodden, my socks were nowhere to be seen.

When I was dressed, he grabbed me by my coat, marched me to the door, unhooked the chain and threw the door open. Jessy was barking again, jumping up at Prendergast's leg.

Down, bitch! he snapped, kicking at her again, catching her on her muzzle. She yelped and darted off upstairs.

Go on, he said, pulling me to the door. He stank. I tried to push him off me but he gripped my coat harder and with his other hand shoved me outside.

If I ever see you back round here, he said, I'll fucking kill you.

With that he slammed the door, and I was left in the freezing night.

The Jensen was still parked down by the terraces. I ran to the car, but even before I got there I could see Eadie wasn't inside though she'd left it unlocked, the keys still in the ignition. I opened the door and threw myself in, away from the icy night air. I sat in the driving seat, shivering, my body out of control. I put my hands on the steering wheel, gripped the wheel as if doing that could stop the shaking.

Walk away, he'd said. Walk away and don't stop walking until the thing that's pulling you down, the thing that'll kill you, is so far behind you it can never find you. Walk away, that's what I thought I could do. Walk away from dreams. Walk away from truths I didn't want to accept. Walk and walk until everything was good and fine. But as I sat gripping the steering wheel, I knew that there was no way I could walk away from what I was facing. To walk you need time.

# Twenty-One

The hawk was waiting for me at the top of High Street. I knew it would be there. When I turned on to the hill and drove up to Great Budworth, I felt like something was pulling me up the hill, like a magnet dragging me from the core of my being up past my house and towards the church. It was morning, the sky crisp in its brightness. The world suddenly felt warm, like all the ice was finally thawing.

There was the hawk, static and locked in place above the sandstone tower of the church. I parked right outside the pub, not taking my eyes off the bird.

I could see my hawk clearly now in the daylight. Its wings were stretched wide, the feathers at its wingtips like fingers splayed out. There was white on its underside, greyish black at the end of its wings and tail. Its talons were yellow and grasped only air. Its head looked almost like it was wearing a hood, a colour so similar to the sandstone of the church it might have been born from that stone. Maybe that was why it was so immobile. It wasn't a hawk. It was a statue thrown free from the church, caught somehow by the sky, and held there only for me to witness.

I walked closer to the church, watching my hawk, refusing to look away. The hawk flickered. For a moment the space around it seemed to quiver and the body of the hawk buffeted like a failing download. I thought it was going to vanish, leave me. I even stretched my arm towards it as if I could stop that happening, catch it, hold onto it.

But the hawk didn't vanish. When the shiver righted itself, I saw the hawk's wings move slowly downwards, beating against the prison of stillness. I think I cried out with a kind of joy. It was free. It could fly. Wings rose, fell, faster. It was hovering now as it should have always been hovering. Then I heard it cry. That was such a beautiful sound because it told me this hawk was real. It had voice. It screeched again.

Fly, I shouted, because I think I was scared that if it didn't take this opportunity to fly right there and then, it might be thrown back into the cell of constancy. Unfixed, I wanted it to fly far from the possibility of being caged in inertia ever again.

Do it, I shouted. I didn't care who might hear me, didn't care if Eadie was watching from her window or if her dad was standing at the church door, my shouts giving proof to his fears. Just fly, I called.

The hawk called back. A screaming song. It turned on its wing and soared away from the church towards the top end of the village. I didn't want it to go. Now it was released, I wanted to see it fly, to know it was a truth beyond my own imaginings. I ran after the hawk, stumbling more than once because I wouldn't look away. I saw it dive low into a field, so I ran from the road through an open gate, my foot breaking through a puddle of ice into the cold mud below. The hawk soared up, then dived again and soared higher. It wasn't hunting, I knew that. It was dancing, it was living, enjoying the freedom that had been offered. I screamed at the hawk to keep flying, to not stop, to go, go. And then it flickered.

There must have been other sounds. The distant roll of cars. The light breeze through the leafless trees. The waking cows moaning. But as my hawk flickered it seemed a void had swallowed the world and there was nothing, no sound, no motion. I froze too. I watched as, mid-dive, my hawk became utterly still. A hanging statue again.

I shouted something, I don't know what. I just know

I screamed out. But there was no sound, just my mouth opening, my desperation evaporating into that new void.

The hawk was motionless.

I knew the runner was there before I saw him. I knew that the minute I looked down from my numbed hawk, I'd see the runner in his eighties tracksuit, caught in that perpetual act of running.

I refused to look, but in the same way as the magnet of the hawk had dragged me up High Street, I felt the pull of the runner's presence forcing me to see him.

I looked away from the hawk. The runner was standing right in front of me.

I hadn't realised last time how young he was. I think I'd taken him for older because, just like in old films, his clothes and even his hairstyle made him seem older. But now I saw his skin wasn't wrinkled, his eyes were open with a twinkle of optimism that was echoed in the smile that was caught on his face. Whoever he was, to run was his joy. I could see that now. Just as the hawk's joy was to hunt, so the runner's joy was to be out there on a field with all the possibility of the world beneath his feet.

Run, I said.

I stepped closer.

Run, I said, louder this time.

I wanted to grab him, shake him, force him out of that entrapment and make him run as the hawk had flown.

Run! I screamed at him.

There was a rush of air like a train racing along a subway. It was ice-cold air. It brought with it a sound of faraway thunder. The runner flickered.

Run! I screamed again.

The air buffeted my body so that I staggered forward towards him. My arm should have touched his, connected, but instead the presence of my arm caused him to flicker, and my arm simply passed through his. He flickered again, his form slatted, cut at. And then he was gone.

Roslin, said a voice. Who are you talking to mate?

I reached out my hand to where the runner had been. Was that his voice? Did he know me? I touched only empty air.

Mate, are you okay?

I turned. Toby was standing by the gate. He looked out of breath, like he'd run to be there.

Where've you been, Roslin? he said, his voice cautious.

He was standing away from me like I was some wild animal he wasn't sure he could approach.

I followed it, I said, pointing up to the too-blue sky.

Toby looked up too but I knew what he saw. Just the

253

vast winter sky, the sun burning to wake at the horizon. No hawk.

It's okay, he said, frowning into the sun. Come on, you come with me now. We'll get you home.

I saw them, I said.

He came forward, no caution. I don't know why but I felt right then like I might just fall off the earth, slip away into the air, fall and fall like nothing was anchoring me. I felt myself sway. Was that how it felt for the runner and the hawk, to suddenly be freed? Was it dizzying? Was it too much? Was that why they'd left so quickly?

I feel sick, I said.

I must have fallen then. Not up away from the earth but into Toby's arms. I felt him catch me.

Easy, Roslin, I heard him say. I've got you.

Did I ever mention how much I hate dreams? I think that was a lie because the dream I had then was something I could never hate.

I was the runner. I was running through endless fields, but I wasn't alone. I was with Eadie, and she was running beside me, sometimes we were even holding hands. I'm not crazy, I don't love Eadie. I know what the dream was. It was a kind of gift, offering me, even if it was just a dream and just for a flash of a life, the chance to believe I might one

254

day love someone and be content to just run with them as if there was nothing else in the world. I think the hawk was there too. Every now and then, I would hear a cry, knew it was calling to me, but when I looked up the sun would be too bright so I'd shield my eyes and maybe there within the glare I'd see wings like oars beating against the bright. Then I'd feel Eadie's hand take me, pull me on, hear her voice say my name and I'd run and run and run with her.

I could have stayed in that dream forever, but the terrible thing was that I woke.

My throat was dry. I coughed and felt someone put a glass to my lips. Water washed over my raw tongue and soothed my throat. It felt like I hadn't drunk for days.

Back with me, Roslin, said Toby.

I need to go home, I said because I remembered where I'd been when I'd fallen. I believed that I was still in the field, that only minutes had passed.

You are home, said Toby. Do you think I'd leave you out there? Drink up.

I did drink up. I'd never been so thirsty. As he tilted the glass and more water filled my throat, I grabbed at the glass. I wanted it all.

Whoa there, said Toby. Don't overdo it.

I shook my head. It's fine. I just need water.

But he pulled the glass away. You need to take it easy, that's what you need to do. That was some deep sleep. You had me worried.

I shook my head again. No, it wasn't. He was wrong. I'd been asleep for minutes, nothing more.

I tried to sit up and as I did, I realised I was in my bed. My body was stiff as if it had been stuck in one position too long, my neck aching.

I don't feel good, I said. How long did I sleep for?

I moved my legs, but they were full of pins and needles.

You shouldn't have let me sleep so long, I said.

Let you? Do you know how many times I tried to wake you? Anyway, they said it was best to just give you whatever time you needed.

Who said?

Foresight Nickson, said Toby. They told me this was normal, to be expected even. They said it might even help, that I was to let you sleep even if it was for days.

Days? But I don't…

No, don't worry. You didn't sleep that long.

I forced myself to sit up more. The curtains in my bedroom were drawn so I had no idea what time of day it was.

Toby put his hand on my arm. Now come on, Roslin, don't get upset. Just take your time.

I pushed his hand away.

How long, Toby?

He sighed and rubbed at the stubble that he didn't have when he'd found me on the field.

A while, he said.

How many days?

Leo, he said. I don't want you to be upset.

Please, just tell me.

He scratched at his cheek. Shook his head. Okay, okay. It was six days, Leo. You slept for six days.

He might as well have told me I'd slept my life away.

# Twenty-Two

There's a song called *O Holy Night*. It's a carol and begins soft, steady in its gentle lulling beauty. I don't usually let hymns or religious songs impact me because I think that's part of the mania of religion, isn't it? All those songs and prayers, all those people singing in unison, that's a way of tricking you into belief because when you hear them, you're almost lifted somewhere else away from the everyday, so you make the mistake of thinking that somewhere else is holy, godly and real. The extra, added-on beauty of the language of religions that makes you forget that you're really singing to silence, that you're praying to no one. Whenever I hear a carol, I try to remember that truth. They're lullabies really, nonsense. They can't influence me because their words, the holy and the saviours and births and the wonder of stars, are lies. But there's a point in *O Holy Night* where I can't stop myself feeling this tug of belief even though I know I could never fully believe. It's when the key shifts and the carol almost commands you as the words command you. It tells you to fall on your knees, to hear the angel voices. Every time I hear that, the words almost pull me down, as if the singular word *fall* is enough to force me on to my knees, prostrate, worshipping a God I know isn't even there.

Eadie was singing *O Holy Night* as I came into the church. She was standing at the foot of the altar, looking down the aisle, but I don't think she could see me. The church was full, mostly with children in Belmont blazers and their parents. Eadie's dad was sat up on the altar in his full vicar costume. If Eadie didn't see me, he certainly saw me as soon I came in, I know he did, but he didn't flinch, didn't lose this serene, benevolent smile that told his parishioners he was within God's glory. I walked up the aisle and took a seat in a pew at the very back of the church. All that time I sat there I could feel his eyes on me, this unholy hatred bubbling within him that he couldn't release unless, I knew, that release was targeted at me or any boy who would ever come near Eadie.

As Eadie sang, she looked up at the vaulted ceiling. I looked up too. The beams were ribs, they reminded me of the bow of a ship, like some Viking longboat had been upturned above us.

Fall on your knees, she sang, her pitch changing.

I gripped the bench. I wasn't going to fall, I knew I wasn't but that word in that song was like a hook jolting me forwards. Eadie's voice wasn't beautiful. It was just enough. It cracked a little, didn't quite meet the right note, but as she kept singing, I couldn't help imagining that her fragility, that quivering voice, was because of worry. Was she worried about me? Was she always worried about Becca?

I imagined telling her what I knew. Taking her to the house. Finding the bracelet. She'd be like the hawk, suddenly freed, and you know what, I'd just let her fly. I wouldn't want to fly with her, I'd just let her go because if I could do that one good thing, free her of that crippling ignorance, then I think I could accept all the rest. The slowing down. The stopping. The forever sleep. I think I could sleep a really deep sleep if I knew she had what she wanted. That would be living, wouldn't it?

I didn't wait for her singing to end. I stood up, walked outside into the fading twilight. There was snow again that night but it seemed even colder than all the days that had gone before. The snow that had settled over the last week was melting and the ice on the roads thawing, but their influence had somehow burrowed deeper into the village so as I stood in the churchyard, kicking my feet at the last of

260

the stubborn snow, I could feel the ice of the world finding its way into my coat, through my jeans, beneath my shirt, past my skin and into my bone. It felt familiar. It felt natural.

Eadie didn't come to me until all the parishioners had left. When the doors opened, I waited until the last family had paraded past her dad, each parishioner shaking his hand as he shared some words about the weather or Christmas with them. Every now and again he would glance my way, still smiling. Eadie came out last. I watched as she talked to her dad, their voices low, restrained. Eventually she put her hand on his and said something I couldn't hear. He looked to me with his jaw set, and nodded to her.

When Eadie came to me, I swear I almost heard the echo of that word. *Fall.* As if she had carried it with her beyond the church's cold acoustics, beyond the lifeless stone, and breathed it at me, not even a whisper just a breath, for me alone to hear.

I didn't fall.

I found Becca, I said, before Eadie could speak in her usual tumbling exuberance.

You found her? she said. What do you mean? In that horrible house?

No, Eadie, there was nothing of Becca's there, I said. I took her hand, but she pulled it away.

Yes, there was, that's why you were gone so long. I waited for you, even when I saw him come back, I still waited because I knew you'd find something. Did you speak to him? Did he tell you what he did? I'm sorry I didn't help you; I was just so scared if you want to know the truth. The minute I saw his car pulling up and that ugly little dog jump out, I had these terrible images in my head of what he'd done to Becca, how he'd done it, but it wasn't Becca he was doing it to, it was me. Leo, I'm sorry I ran away like a coward, I'm sorry I left you there. What happened? Did he hurt you?

Her hand took mine.

It's okay, I said. Nothing happened. He didn't do anything to me, Eadie. I don't think he's what you thought he was. I mean he's a mess but he's no killer.

She was frowning. I could tell she didn't want to believe what I was saying. She'd believed her own truth for so long because it had been her only answer. Becca hadn't run away. Prendergast had hurt Becca. She could help her sister by making everyone know what Prendergast had done. It was too fixed in her like a splinter that had gone in too deep, so it was a black line beneath her skin. And here I was, about to pull that splinter out before it festered anymore.

You're not making sense, she said. He must have hurt her,

there must have been something in there. Did he threaten you or something? Is that it? It's okay, once we tell the police what you found he can't hurt you or me or anyone ever again.

I squeezed her hand. It's not like that, I said. Prendergast didn't hurt Becca; you have to believe me. I can prove it.

I pulled on her hand to lead her out of the churchyard as her dad watched us intently and uncomfortably, but she wouldn't budge. I saw her dad fold his arms, desperate to come over and separate us.

Please just come with me, I said.

Her head did that tilt. I didn't know then if she'd pull her hand away, turn, go back to her dad or if she'd trust me. Why should she? We hardly knew each other. I was a weirdo. I was a stranger who she'd just happened to kiss.

How do you know? she said. I felt her arm relax, the need to pull away lessen.

Kismet, I said.

I pulled on her hand and this time she let herself move with me. We walked away from the church, up Westage Lane and then on to Heath Lane towards the house I was sure now was Ed Bray's house.

When we got to the house, I noticed something I hadn't seen before. There was a *For Sale* sign poking up over the wall, not a single light on inside the house, all the curtains open so it looked hollow and unloved in its solitude.

We stood outside the empty house, and I felt her hand slip out of mine.

Do you know what I've just realised? she said.

That you don't know me.

She smiled. Oh, I already knew that. No, it's more that ever since I first saw you, I felt like you were temporary, like you wouldn't be around that long, and I had this strange feeling that because of that I needed to know you before you vanished.

Like a ghost.

No, don't be so dark. More like a rainbow, something that when you notice it already seems to be fading so you look at it and know that you just need to experience it before it fades completely. Have you ever heard of a green flash?

I've heard of the Flash, I said.

Ugh, I don't believe in superheroes. A green flash is real, silly. Last year we lived in Botswana for a couple of months. Dad was invited by the bishop because our churches are sister churches or something like that. It's beautiful there, everything feels more real, like the world there is living in a different way to it is here. Here it feels like we're always waiting for winter but there it felt like there never would be a winter. We were having a barbeque at the bishop's house which was right in the middle of this massive desert. Nothing else for miles. I was drinking a Coke looking at the sunset. African suns are different too. I feel like you see the sun there and understand that it's just one big fire, that it's burning and won't ever stop burning. The sky was orange, and the desert was orange. It made me feel a bit sick, like all the world was on fire. Then there was this flash of green right above the sun just as it was almost set. Just a tiny flash, then gone. I sat outside on the porch in this stupid rocking chair just staring at the exact spot where I'd seen the flash. I sat there for ages, but I never saw another. I've never seen one since. Not one. I've tried and tried, watched about a thousand sunsets, and never seen one single crappy flash. I don't think I will. You're like that flash, not there then suddenly there. I keep thinking that I have to not let you vanish. Is that mad? Do I sound like a psycho nutter stalker? I don't mean I'm obsessed with you or anything, it's not that. It's just when I first saw you watching me, I got this funny feeling that I needed to know you, that I couldn't just let you pass by, disappear. Is that nuts?

I kissed her.

I wanted to be able to tell her that she was a phenomenon too. I tried to think of one that fitted her. I thought of lights. The aurora borealis. Light pillars. A sun dog. Not a Brocken spectre, a bright spectre, not my shadow playing tricks on me but a projection of an impossible future, what might have been, the impossible made possible. I wanted to tell her that she was the truest experience I'd ever had, that everything else had been lies, echoes, phantoms, and myths. That she'd been real, and I was grateful for that. That when we were in her room, I'd never felt so untethered. That she was unexpected, unpredictable, and unforgettable. That I was happy, even though I really was as temporary as she imagined I was, because when I was gone at least she'd still be here. But I'm not Toby. I'm not a poet. All I could do was kiss her.

Usually, people remember their first kiss. Usually, it's your first kiss that's the most intense, the one you judge all other kisses against, the one that makes you understand what all the fuss was about. As I kissed Eadie, I knew something that a lot of people probably never know. That kiss we shared outside Ed Bray's empty house was my last kiss. I knew that as our lips touched, as the world was cast away from us, as all sound ceased, all movement slowed, as there was only our kiss and nothing else. I knew that and I was okay with that knowledge. I didn't try to make the kiss last. It was enough just to kiss her and pull away. A brief perfection.

That was ballsy, she said, letting go of my hand. I didn't think you were that ballsy.

I must have been right then, I said. You don't know me.

She punched me lightly on my arm. Yeah right.

The house had been there as we kissed. An ominous sentinel waiting for us to remember it existed. I saw Eadie look to its red brick and bay windows, her face changing. She looked scared. I think that was the only time I'd ever seen her look scared.

Here then, she said.

I think so, I said.

She crossed her arms. How do you know?

I looked up the drive and saw the garage. The same garage with the same roller shutters and the door beside the shutters, the one Ed Bray had used. I looked at the drive. The same shale. I thought of Becca's bracelet falling to the drive.

I don't know, I said. But it happened here. Wait here, I'll prove it.

I looked at her. Of course, I wanted to kiss her again, maybe I even thought that a kiss would reassure her, calm her fear. That's arrogant, isn't it? But I didn't kiss her, I just took her hand and looked her right in the eye, told her that she didn't have to worry anymore, that all I had to do was

267

go inside the garage and then it would all be done, that she could stop, that she could live. Even then I still wanted to kiss her, but I know why I didn't. I wanted that last kiss to be original, to exist forever because there was only that last kiss. If I'd caved in and kissed her again then I'd ruin that originality. It would become a copy, an echo, and it would die through that echoing.

I left her standing on the pavement, her arms folded against the night's cold. I walked up the drive to the garage.

Kismet can't be real, serendipity or luck can't really exist, but something was on my side that night because the garage door was unlocked. I turned the handle, it opened, and I went inside. There was no light inside the garage, so I took out my phone and used the torch to scan the space. There was no car parked up, but the garage was full of boxes covered in dustsheets and the shelves that ran around the walls were packed with tins of paint, tools hanging from nails, old copies of *Auto Trader*, boxes labelled with words like 2004 Invoices, Insurance and Malaga 1997. I went around the garage pulling sheets away, as if I'd find the bracelet just waiting for me. Something made me turn. It felt like cold fingers tracing down my back, like the world had suddenly and subtly been shaken. I turned, my torchlight illuminating the far corner of the garage. Ed was there.

He looked as I'd seen him that night. The same clothes, the same neatly trimmed beard. The only difference was that he was wearing gloves, yellow marigolds. I knew he couldn't see me but still I lowered my torch. He was standing over a battered trunk. I watched as he lifted the trunk and stared inside. He stood there, holding the lid open, and I could hear him breathing hard, beads of sweat on his shaven head. I think I knew what was in the trunk.

Holding the lid open with one hand, his free hand went into his pocket and brought out the bracelet. I could see the bracelet more clearly. A chain of little silver beads and then a little bee, its body yellow and blue, its wings the same silver as the beads. I watched as Ed tossed the bracelet into the trunk. He didn't do it with any reverence or respect. He threw like it was rubbish, like he was glad to be rid of it and then he slammed the lid down hard.

Where do ghosts come from and where do they go once they've haunted you? The vision of Ed Bray disappeared with the slamming of that lid, but I could still feel his presence in that space, oppressive with a weight of guilt. It made the garage feel smaller, like it was closing in trying to crush itself to escape the memory of what had happened there. I didn't want to imagine how Becca's life had ended, but I couldn't fight off the flashes of what could have happened.

Becca shouting at him. Him hitting her. There were so many tools in the garage, hammers, chisels, heavy wrenches. I saw her falling, no more shouting. I don't think he would have panicked; I don't think he would have cared. I imagined him methodically lifting her body into the trunk and then going about cleaning the space of any evidence. That was what the marigolds had been for. In the end all he had left to dispose of was the bracelet.

The trunk had vanished with the ghost of Ed.

In its place was an outline of where that trunk must have stood for years, a shadow stain.

My proof was gone. My promise to Eadie was a lie.

There was an empty Dulux paint can on the floor so I kicked it as hard as I could, sent it flying across the garage where it struck a brush that was leaning against the wall. The brush wobbled then fell and hit an old car battery.

I don't know why any of that made me see the iPhone. It was on a low shelf above the battery. Maybe my arm moved, the torch's beam jumping up to shine on that exact shelf at that exact moment when I was accepting there was nothing I could do to help Eadie. Maybe it was kismet.

I crossed the garage and picked up the old iPhone. At first, I'd only noticed the colour. Yellow and blue. I hadn't seen the letter B because the phone had been left face-down on the shelf. How had Ed missed that? Had his arrogance, his lack of emotion, led him to sloppiness? Or maybe he'd kept it as some kind of sick prize in the same way Eadie had believed Prendergast would.

The phone case was striped like a bee and the letter B encrusted in its centre sparkled with glitter. I turned the case over, pressing the power button as I did but it was predictably dead. The front screen was shattered, a spider web emanating out from a point in the middle of the screen and I wondered if that point of shattering had echoed another point of shattering, if it happened in whatever last moment of violence Becca had experienced at the hands of Ed Bray. There, in the corner of the phone where one of the strands of cracking touched the case, I could see something, a stain, dried, stuck to the screen. A liquid that had been spilt on the phone and never wiped away. I knew what it was.

As I held the case, I felt my hand twitch. It was like somehow the tendons in my wrist had suddenly severed, like a guitar string snapping with a twang. I looked at my hand and I knew what was about to happen. The single twitch became a little shiver which grew quickly into a trembling that pulsed up my hand into my fingers. I was holding the phone, I could see that, but I could no longer feel the phone. I knew right then, and I don't think I knew it till then, that this wasn't new. My fit in front of Eadie's dad hadn't been the first. This tremble was old, had been with me for too long. How many times had that tremble turned into my whole body shaking itself apart? How many times had it shifted into my body locking itself, gripping a child's arm and not hearing the child's cries? But as my hand shook, I felt something else. I felt almost like I wasn't part of the world. It reminded me of old episodes of *Star Trek*, the ones Dad used to watch on the Sci-Fi Channel, where the crew would transport and their bodies would shimmer with fractured light, distort, little galaxies bursting within the mist of transporting, and then the ghost-figures would disappear. In the show they'd be transported back to the safety of their spaceship, but I understood that my body wasn't phasing out to somewhere safer. It was more like a television image becoming lost, distorting, failing, until the screen turned itself black and there was no longer any image at all.

I grabbed my wrist, held it hard.

No, I said. Not now.

I gripped my wrist as tightly I could. The phone kept shaking in my grip but the harder I held myself, the more that spasm slowed until the phone was calmed.

I kept squeezing the phone in my hand, as if any slackening of that grip might awaken another convulsion. I walked slowly to the garage door and outside. Eadie was standing at the end of the drive, but I couldn't look at her as I walked towards her. I knew that what I was about to give her would help her, free her, but I knew it would crush her too. It was the beginning of a terrible answer, and I was the one carrying that answer. I'd give her the phone and she'd tell her dad. Her dad would know he was wrong. His daughter hadn't disowned her family, run away at to find a new life. Maybe that had been an easy narrative for Eadie's dad to live with. Now he'd have to face the truth, Eadie too. Ed Bray had killed Becca. There was no selfish new life. There was no Becca somewhere halfway across the world, free of her dad's judgement. The police would come to Ed Bray's house and maybe they'd arrest him. Maybe he'd tell them where he'd taken that trunk. Maybe he'd admit to everything. It would take time, months maybe, but Eadie and her dad would have an answer to where Becca was, and it would all start with that phone. A broken screen. A mark of blood. Becca's bee and her B. I knew I wouldn't see any of that play out but as I walked down the drive, looking down at the shale, I knew it would play out until Becca's death wasn't a buried secret anymore. Eadie would know. Her dad would know. Everyone would know. And I'd be gone, unable to go to Eadie and ask if I'd done the right thing, if I was right to give her that case, if she was happy.

What is it? said Eadie. What's that in your hand, Leo?

I'm sorry, I said.

I held out the phone with the back facing up. I watched as she frowned, studied the case, saw the sparkle of the B, the bee striping, saw the realisation hit her, saw her fall apart inside as she grabbed the phone.

It's hers, she said. It's hers. This was hers Leo.

It was in the garage, I said. There was a man who lived here. His name was Ed Bray.

She looked at me. What do you mean? How do you know that?

I'm sorry, I said. I wished I could have taken her back into the garage with me, wished that the ghost or vision of Ed Bray would return so she could see I wasn't mad. But I knew that she could never share in that. Those apparitions were my own. I didn't understand how they were my own, why I was seeing a past I was never a part of, but I knew that it was all because of one thing. The closer I got to the twentieth December, the more my brain was tumbling reality and the imagined, the impossible and the remembered together, and the more it all mixed up the more it all fell apart. Everything was fragmenting.

Leo, she said. Is she in there?

I moved to hold her hand but when our hands touched she didn't hold mine back.

She's gone, I said. I squeezed her hand, but she only stared at me, her face drained, her eyes wide as she tried to rationalise what everything meant.

She's gone, she said.

I nodded. I think you need to go home, I said. Your dad needs to see this. Come on, I'll walk you.

She didn't answer. We walked slowly back into Great Budworth, neither of us saying a word. It had started to snow again, just a light drift. Everything was quiet. When we passed the pub, I looked inside. I could see people, see the light of the fire, see the Christmas tree ringed with flickering lights, but everything seemed too still. We walked past the church, the graveyard. I glanced up, but through the drifting snow I could see no hawk. When we got to Eadie's house, I was sure I'd say something, but when I looked at her, she was looking down at the phone's broken screen, as if she were seeing her own private apparition there in the cracks. I knocked on her front door.

Time isn't time. A day can be a year or a second. I know

that now. If you hold something in a moment you can make it last forever. Like a kiss you don't want to end. Like childhood, the way you don't believe that it will ever end and then the rush of years from the day you put your toys away, when you tell yourself you're not a kid anymore. It races then, you can't stop it racing. Like the clock in our living room Dad got for however many years of work. When I wake from sleeping on the couch, I can always hear its ticking. I look at the clock and see the ache of its hand inching forward, and because there's nothing else but waking I watch the hand move so slowly that I'm sure a minute must be an hour and wonder why I ever worried about not having enough time. Like a runner being suddenly aware of their leg rising, falling, their own movement, almost as if they stop themselves in the act of running, a leg hanging, between the movement on and the movement before. Or a hawk, aware that time doesn't matter. It can hover in the air for a day if it needs. Its movements unseen. A frozen thing. A life beyond time. Watching, waiting, seeing. As I stood on Eadie's doorstep, our hands still together though now she had wrapped her fingers lightly around mine, there was no time. We didn't speak. Her thoughts were somewhere else. But we were together in that moment and time had no remit. Time couldn't intrude like it always wanted to.

I think I let go of her hand as the door opened. I think letting go of her hand let time back in, and her dad was there then, seeing his daughter with tears in her eyes, seeing me beside her and hating me.

What's he done? he snapped, going to Eadie, pulling her into him.

Her body fell into her dad's. Not him, she said, sobbing. Becca. It's this, it's hers.

She wriggled free of his embrace and held the phone to him.

The B was his daughter's name. It shined up at him so he couldn't not see it, the glitter alive and glinting.

I walked away. I don't think they even noticed I was gone, though maybe Eadie did eventually, maybe she turned and saw me walking back towards the church, maybe she thought about calling me, maybe she even moved to go after me but her dad gently stopped her. Maybe.

I didn't hurry home. The truth is, I was exhausted. My legs were concrete blocks dragging me down. The world felt heavy. I felt like I could sleep and never wake. Now I wasn't holding Eadie's hand, I'd grabbed hold of my wrist again because with every step I could feel it tremble. Holding my arm did no good. By the time I was at my front door, the hand holding the wrist was shaking too. My arms were shivering. I could feel my head nodding. Every part of me felt like it wanted to tear itself away and say no, we're not ready, you go, you sleep, we'll be fine, we're not ready, I told you we're not.

I managed to open the front door but the simple act of doing that tore away the last shreds of energy I had. My eyes closed and I felt myself falling forwards. I suppose I must have fallen heavily but as it happened it felt slow. There was no pain when my head smacked against the hall tiles. I felt like I was falling on a cushion. I know Toby was there, I could hear him though what he was saying was too far away for me to understand. I don't think I cared about what he was saying. I was happy to stay there on the floor, to sleep. I couldn't feel the tremors anymore, but I knew they were happening in every cell of my body. Wherever I was, there was a contentedness, a new calm that might be called stillness.

I'm okay, I said.

# *Twenty-Three*

I heard Toby's voice and I remembered Toby's voice. All the poems he'd ever read to me, wanted me to understand. Or maybe he was speaking those words again, trying to find some connection that would pull me back to him. It wouldn't work. I was far away and drifting further from him with every fragment he spoke. I heard him say the words and I became the words. They found a way into my sleep and as he spoke, they seemed to form all that was left of me. He said I was a small boat alone on dark water, that the boat was lifting me in its manifold arms. Toby spoke and his words were like small gods falling into me. Everything was confused and echoing. He spoke the words and I imagined the words. He spoke the words and I saw them. My life was within a falling leaf. But it was winter, and all the leaves were dead. Was that my thought or another's words? Nothing was original, everything was copied. I was turned on a lathe where replica became real but even that wasn't a real thought, not my own. Someone else had written it. It was someone else's truth, telling another story. Read, echoed, repeated. I was an echo that needed to stop. I was as small as a world and as large as alone. No, that wasn't me. That was a story that wasn't part of me. Petals clung to a wet black bough, but I wasn't the bough or the petal, I was the listener and that was the poem. It was written before I was born, made, and it would be read after I was gone. Let me go there, I heard Toby say, and I knew that it wasn't him who had to go anywhere. I was alone and I was scared. Let me go then, I said but he couldn't hear me. I felt a hand in my hand and no matter how much I wanted to pull my hand away I couldn't free it. Frozen, I saw a cave with a frozen pool. I was climbing Helvellyn again like when I was fourteen and the black lake in its crater was an eye watching me. I saw Eadie tilt her head, her eyes seeing me like no eyes had ever seen me. I felt the wind then, cold upon my all. I wished I could banish the air, divide the light but that wasn't my dream. Words attacked me. I wanted to tell Toby to stop, to let me sleep, stop, but he kept reading, kept pulling me back. I shivered without moving. It was too cold always, and I was much too far out all my life. I knew that one, remembered

Toby reading it to Mum, her crying. Starlit even, whatever else is silence. That sounded beautiful but I didn't recognise the words. How many poems did he have for me? Bridges built with slow recitals, each line and stanza another step closer to reaching me. For a long time then everything was silent, but I knew there were ignorant armies within me clashing through a thousand nights. He said those last words softly, as if they meant so much to him. I could hear swords, steel on steel, and cries, tears on tears. I woke but did not wake. I saw Toby but he didn't see me. I said Eadie's name a million times but all I saw was Becca hitting Ed Bray's chest, screaming at him, and he wasn't a man. He was a hawk. He was searching for prey. I was running away from him. I was myself and I was Becca, and I was Eadie. I felt someone kiss me and the kiss made me stop running. Em was there, dressing, saying sorry over and over. I told her she should no longer mourn for me when I am dead. I was a sullen bell. I was sweet thoughts forgotten. I was a broken verse. I told her to let the memory of me decay with my life. Senescence was beginning and there were borders left to cross. None of those words, thoughts, were mine because there was no me. I was a fake, a copy. Even my subconscious was just a mess of lines fed into me, spoken with someone else's voice, written with someone else's hand. False. I ran on.

I've always hated dreams. I hated them right up until that long sleep because it was in that dream that Eadie walked with me and how could I ever hate that?

When I knew she was there, I think we'd already been walking for days.

What do you think that is? she asked.

She was shielding her eyes against the low sun, looking to our right where there was a line of farm buildings and above those a tall, thin needle rising high into the clear air.

It's an aerial, I said.

Oh, do you think it's so tall because its signal needs to travel further?

I looked at the aerial. It was so thin it looked almost like someone had tried to slice a line down the fabric of reality.

Maybe it's to listen to everyone at once, I said.

She elbowed me in my side. You're a weirdo, Weirdo. Who thinks like that? Nah, I bet it's meant to carry signals where no other signal can go. Do you think it'd take a signal to where you're going?

I followed the subtle line of the aerial up into the vast sky. There were no clouds at all. High up, the blue of the sky became smudged with white as if the very air was fading out, unreal and only imagined.

I don't think any signal goes that far, I said.

Eadie was looking up too. You sound like my dad. He doesn't think God can hear us unless we're praying. I bet he wouldn't think you could send a radio signal to heaven or even just message heaven. You shouldn't be like that, Leo. You should be more optimistic. Go on, be optimistic. Say, Eadie, I won't need a signal to hear you.

I moved closer to her. She was wearing her Belmont uniform and I remembered it was summer, that I'd met her after school like I did every Friday but this time I'd brought a picnic, that we were going to the mere.

Eadie, I said. I won't need a signal to hear you.

She laughed. You're so obedient. I'm glad I won't need one though. Do you think I could whisper, and you'd hear me?

Eadie, I said. You could whisper and I'd hear you.

She laughed again. Thank you.

For what?

You know what. All that stuff with Becca. I wish you'd known me after that, God I changed. I was tense and angsty when you met me, probably didn't let you get a word in edgeways I was so manic. I never told anyone the truth, not even Dad, but from the day Becca left I felt like I was trapped, like I was in this big block of ice, and it was just getting more and more frozen as the years went on until it

283

was so frozen it was like concrete. It was like an ice prison that I knew I'd never get out of. But then you were there, staring at me like a weirdo, and I could feel it thawing, feel it melting just a little. I was so scared of that prison, I'd started to really believe that if it didn't melt then no matter what came along to make me happy the real me would always be cold, dead even, until I knew what had happened to Becca. And I know now, don't I. I know because of you, Leo. It's so sad you couldn't have seen me after the ice had melted, you would have liked me so much more.

I wanted to tell her that I did see her afterwards, that we did this walk every Friday, that it was summer not winter, that I was there with her, but I knew she was right.

The aerial quivered with the whisper of a breeze.

We were standing very close to each other, both of us watching the aerial tremble, and only when the breeze had passed, and the aerial had stilled itself did I turn to her and move even closer to her and kiss her. I expected her lips to be cold because I knew it wasn't really Eadie but nothing about her was ice. I felt her hand on my back, moving, and I could feel her heart beating and hear her breathing. There was nothing about her that was frozen or locked in place or always unmoving. She had been real and, as we kissed, I realised I had been real too.

# Twenty-Four

When I woke, I kept my eyes closed for a long time because I think I knew it would be their last opening. It wasn't just a sense of some impending doom. It was what my body was telling me. Even as I lay there, I could hear my own ragged breaths and knew the sound they made wasn't right. All of me felt heavy, tired. I almost felt like if the bed hadn't been beneath me my body would have dragged itself down and down through the carpet, through the floor, through the living room beneath and on until I was entombed somewhere and still. Even when I was ready to open my eyes, my eyelids seemed to have forgotten their sole job and as they laboured to open, I thought the room was dark but as my eyes opened fully, I understood that the darkness I saw wasn't because of a lack of light, it was because of the failings of my eyes. A fog of my own making, it lingered all around me.

Toby, I said, a sudden panic in my voice. I'd told myself I was ready. That this was okay. But anyone who tells themselves that must know they're lying. I was scared.

Hey, shush now, Roslin, Toby said. I felt his hand grab mine. It's okay, mate, I'm here. You're not alone.

I don't feel well, I said. Can I ring Mum, please? I just need...

Toby's hand squeezed mine. I felt something warm and wet touch my forehead and knew he was holding a flannel to my skin. Was I hot? I hadn't felt hot. If anything, I felt an absence of either heat or warmth. I think that's what was scaring me. I'd expected pain or discomfort, but as soon as I woke, I could feel this horrible sense of nothing being wrong other than heavy tiredness.

I know you need them, said Toby. But you don't need to ring them, mate. Can't you see them? They're here, Roslin. Of course they're bloody here.

I tried to lift my head but there was no chance of that. I looked for my parents, moved my head left then right as best as I could, but though I knew Toby was right there next to me I couldn't even see him.

They're not, I said. I heard my own voice slur, a slow struggle.

We are, Leo, said another voice. I felt a weight on the bed. I felt a hand on my cheek that was light and familiar.

Mum, I said.

Her hand moved to my hair. You don't need to worry, she said. I'm here now. I'm sorry I wasn't here sooner. You're my best boy, Leo.

I felt her hand stroke my hair and then I knew there was someone else in the room. A bigger presence, a faint smell of oil and the odd secret cigarette Mum never knew about.

Dad, I said, pulling my hand from Toby's and searching for my Dad's. At last, I felt him take my hand, squeeze it hard, then I felt his head on my chest and I heard something I'd never heard before. I heard my dad crying.

You're my son, he said. You're my boy, Leo. You've always been my boy; do you hear me? I want you to know that we always loved you, that nothing was ever different. You were our son, Leo, ours.

I did hear him. I did believe him, but I was so tired that all I wanted to do was go back to sleep. I didn't mind so much what that sleep meant. I just needed to sleep.

As I lay there, I remembered being little and Mum singing to me. There were so many songs, most of them I could never remember, but there was one I'd never forget. I wanted her to sing it for me.

Echo, I managed to say.

What did he say? I heard Toby ask.

I felt Mum move her hand to take my free hand. He said echo, she said. Is that what you want, Leo? Do you want me to sing to you?

I nodded, slurred yes though I don't think the sound I made was really a word.

When Mum began to sing, I closed my eyes. The fog was gone and in its place was a deep black that wasn't frightening. I could still hear her voice. *Little Sir Echo, how do you do*. I lay there, her words growing fainter and fainter, the awareness of Dad's hand holding my hand lessening. The knowledge that Toby was there watching me, fading. I could feel myself pulling away from them all. I heard Mum's words as if they were coming to me from the long-ago past, from my childhood. *My* childhood.

But you're always so far away, away, she sang. *Away* repeating until it was barely a whisper then gone.

I was running. The field I ran upon was endless but there was no effort in running forever. Above me I heard a cry and looking up into the clear sky I saw my hawk. The hawk wasn't still or stuck in place. It was free, flying as I ran, and I knew as I ran that I would never stop running just as my hawk would never stop flying.

## *End*